To Patricia, my wife, whose great beauty inside and out, and love have given me a new start in life.

THE WAR COMES HOME

John Hansen

Red City Reviews Rates This Book:

FOUR STARS

"The first installment of The Bluesuit Chronicles is a compelling start to what is sure to be an epic saga. Former Golden Gloves boxer and Army medic Roger Hitchcock returns home from Vietnam to a different America than the one he left. His hometown ballooned in size during his absence and the police force needs to expand… Like his fellow veterans who pin on the badge, they find that when they left Vietnam, Vietnam didn't leave them. Now they go from being called 'baby killers' to being called 'pigs' yet they do what they did before, serve and protect an often undeserving public. The drug craze of the early seventies takes a heavy toll on the Boomer generation, and the social fabric begins to unravel. This book is a collection of stories filled to the brim with nail-biting action, romance, and intrigue, which are all based on actual events."

READERS COMMENT ABOUT
BOOK ONE - *THE WAR COMES HOME*

"John- Just finished your first installment of the *The Bluesuit Chronicles*. Enjoyed it immensely! You are a gifted writer that puts the reader right on the scene, and not always safely out of harm's way. Am in the midst of two other books. Yours was easy to pick up, but difficult to put down. As busy as I have been, it was fortunate that I could easily pick up right where I left off without needing to reread past pages. It is a tribute to your style of ever-changing, but connected scenes. I appreciate your style, and truly enjoyed the book. Have always liked a look-back at transitional times in history with a thoughtful perspective of the impact of the period. You framed it well in your Foreword and Author's Note. I like to learn from the books I read, and I have done with yours. Further, both the action and the drama are told in compelling style, and intertwined expertly to bring the reader down from the adrenaline of the chase. Add to that my personal interest in the topic and era, and I have a complete package, and certainly one that left me hungry for more. "

John Schwiesow – Scottsdale, Arizona

"I wish there were more chapters, John. I could not put it down. Not only was it very well written but I began to imagine not only what I would do but how that moment in police work would cope with the different times. Can't wait until the next one."

Officer Nathan Vance – Bonney Lake Police Dept., WA

"John Hansen's way of telling a story takes you 'along for the ride'." Fully a man of honor, he can describe the tough job, a man's personal thoughts and the seedy side of life equally, making you want more!"

Nancy Meyn – Redmond, WA

"An exciting read, riveting action, romance and moving scenes. It took me back to the Bellevue I knew in the 'good old days.' Impossible to put down."

Cynthia Davis – Bellevue, WA

'I so strongly related to *The War Comes Home* that I read it in a single sitting. The descriptions of the police back then, traditional eight-point billed hats and billy clubs, their interactions with each other and the people they protected brought back wonderful memories. I especially related to the action scenes – I felt like I was really there. My only question is – when can I get my hands on the next book?"

Harry Bennett – Phoenix, AZ

Very well written, flows well. I found this book very entertaining and am looking forward to the next Volume. Having lived in the area where it is portrayed, I was able to visualize some of the incident and locations and my curiosity is peaked for the next installment.

Walks Alone

From the minute I started reading The War Comes Home, I couldn't put it down. I was captivated by the balance of action and drama that John Hansen expertly weaves throughout this fast paced historical fiction. I'm looking forward to reading the next one.

S. McDonald

The Bluesuit Chronicles: Book One - The War Comes Home
© 2014 John Hansen
All rights reserved

ISBN: 978-0-9667829-6-7

Published by
LifeGuides Press
Gilbert, AZ 85295
480 703-1244

Cover design by Ira Mandas

Printed in the United States of America

ABOUT THE SYMBOLISM OF THE COVER

We changed the cover to portray main character Roger Hitchcock as a humanitarian warrior with a scene from his service as an Army medic on a Vietnam battlefield. The rife and bayonet in the ground symbolize that it was the war that influenced Hitchcock to enter police work instead of returning to medical school. The cracked earth around him as a policeman symbolizes the divided and polarized state of America when he comes home. The flames below him symbolize the destruction threatening the country.

THE WAR COMES HOME

John Hansen

They left Vietnam when they came home,
but Vietnam never left them.

Yet for an often undeserving public,
they continued to serve and protect…

BOOK ONE of
THE BLUESUIT CHRONICLES

FOREWORD

Like the medieval knights when they returned from the Crusades, Vietnam vets came home to changes in the country they could not have imagined. Not since the Civil War had there been such postwar fallout of colossal change and upheaval: a dramatic rise in violent crime, civil unrest, and bitter cultural polarization. America's police struggled to meet the new challenges.

Those of us who pinned on the badge then didn't know ours was the last generation of the traditional eight-point billed hat, the .38 Special revolver, batons and spring-loaded saps, patrol cars with a single bubblegum red dome on top and a siren activated by flipping a console switch and pressing the horn ring.

Some became cops to do traditional police work: catching burglars and armed robbers. Others did it to hold the line against the degeneration that was sweeping the nation. This is our story.

DEDICATION

This book is fiction based on actual events. Any resemblance to other persons, living or dead, is purely coincidental. It is written in honor of the men and women who added themselves to the "thin blue line" after serving in the Vietnam War. They are the unsung heroes of the Baby Boom generation. Though Vietnam became America's most unpopular war, but they did the right thing anyway—they gave their best years and often their lives to serve. Instead of parades and marching bands at their homecoming they were greeted by scorn and derision, often by people they had grown up with who had refused to answer the call of duty. Their response to the shameful treatment they received was of the highest order: they donned another uniform and continued to serve.

Acknowledgements

This series would not be possible without the help of various retired members of the Bellevue and Seattle Police Departments, who served in uniform during that transitional period of the 1970s. Special thanks to Robert Gavin, who first helped me with initial editing of the text, and to Dee Dees, editor and publisher, who patiently spent even more time and effort with me, editing and formatting this first volume of The Bluesuit Chronicles to get it into ebook and print formats. Finally, and not least, my heartfelt thanks to my longtime friend and high school running mate, artist Ira Mandas for his exceptionally painstaking efforts to produce the excellent and captivating cover design.

AUTHOR'S NOTE

1970—America is coming apart. The war in Vietnam spread into Cambodia; Ohio National Guardsmen shoot down four war protesters at Kent State; the My Lai Massacre in Vietnam rocks the nation; college campuses become hotbeds of violent protest; revolutionary Marxist groups like the Symbionese Liberation Army and the Black Panthers embark on crime sprees involving armed robbery, kidnapping, and murder.

Hollywood, novelists and the news media focus on the action and trials of the big city police departments. After all, that's where all the action was – or was it? FBI statistics for officers killed in the line of duty for the years 1971 through 1974 reveal an under-recognized, and surprising story—*over half* of officers killed in the line of duty were serving in suburban and small town police departments and rural "cow county" sheriff's offices. In point of fact, the risk to officers in the quieter jurisdictions can be greater because the dullness of routine patrol often leads to deadly complacency resulting in crippling injuries or police funerals. It is time the full story is told; hence I present The Bluesuit Chronicles.

John Hansen

1

THE NIGHT OF THE TR6

Under cool Northwest skies smacking of rain, rookie Patrolman Roger Hitchcock prepared for another slow night on patrol. After shift briefing he checked out his black-and-white cruiser, a 1970 Plymouth Fury, factory-equipped with modified engine and suspension. He checked lights, wipers, fluid levels, inside the trunk for emergency supplies and under the seats for hidden evidence or trash.

Next he checked the policeman's ultimate weapon—the pump shotgun, racked butt stock-up on the transmission hump. It had to be "cruiser ready"—chamber empty, safety on, four rounds in the magazine tube. Each round consisted of nine thirty-three caliber lead balls; a single blast is capable of vaporizing human flesh and bone, eliminating barricades, even stopping a car. He moved the seat back to accommodate his six-foot-plus frame, laid his baton on the floor by the driver door, snuggled his eight-cell heavy-duty flashlight (the kind cops sometimes use as a club) on the seat next to his right leg.

Lastly, the young war veteran purposely nudged the butt of his .38 service revolver with his elbow, reassuring himself of its presence in his holster. His dark blue uniform came from the cleaners, fresh and crisp. He liked how he looked in it.

He started the engine and lit a Winston, careful not to drop ashes on his lap as he waited for Ira Walker.

Other third-shift officers rolled single-file from the station, radioing Dispatch they were in service. Tonight Hitchcock would be doubling up with Walker, who was in the station explaining to the sergeant why he came in to work on his night off. Hitchcock knew the reason: Walker's marriage was down for the count and he was taking it hard.

Walker emerged from the station, grim-faced, stress in every step. Hitchcock wanted to tactfully help if he could.

"Come on, crime fighter—while we're young! The bad guys are waitin' for us," jollied Hitchcock. Walker opened the passenger door and got in.

"So what's the latest on the home front?"

"The latest?'" Walker echoed as he shut the door. "The latest, if you can believe it, is that Donna found out when our next cost-of-living increase kicks in, *and* that it will be retroactive. So her attorney wasted no time jacking me up for more bucks. She's already getting the house, child support *plus* maintenance. I'm so broke I can't pay attention. I'm living in the basement of my own home, while she's dating a guy in front of me and my kids, having him in the house."

Hitchcock decided to stay off the topic. Tuesday nights in September were always slow, so both men expected a quiet night working together. It would be like old times. Hitchcock keyed the mike:

"Three Zero Six to Radio."

"Three Zero Six — go."

"10-8, a two-man unit. Walker, P-53, on board."

"Received. Three Zero Six is 10-8, a two-man unit."

At 8:10 p.m. Hitchcock and Walker drove into the night, heading south through light traffic to District Six.

Before the Army, Walker had been a state champion heavyweight wrestler in high school and college. Blondish, average height, his lean physique became a matter of history, owing to a youthful appetite that didn't downsize to adult metabolism. Walker's adult girth and handsome boyish face tempted belligerent drunks and brawlers into fighting him, only to discover his terrible strength, usually via the hospital, making him something of a locker room legend among fellow officers.

"Good thing you're so right at home in Eastgate. The brass plans on keeping you here 'cause they think it's so dead you won't get into trouble," Walker said. "I heard they decided to leave you here … like this is a sort of … Siberia. The citizen complaints when you pulled over six cars at once and wrote them all up for ten miles over the limit during morning rush hour just before your probation was over was almost the last straw. Everybody but the brass laughed."

"Yeah? Well I'm not surprised," Hitchcock grinned happily. "I'm the better for it. What they don't know is I would have chosen District Six if it hadn't been assigned to me. The criminals here are serious crooks — adults, not pansy juvenile punks, or hippy trash wearing the flag on the seat of their pants, like you get in northern districts. I'll take honest, redneck crooks any day."

Hitchcock joined Bellevue PD right after his second tour in Vietnam as an Army medic. Younger and taller than Walker, Hitchcock had lean features, a shock of dark brown hair and high cheek-bones; he was ruddy and flat-stomached, a steel-muscled former boxer and centerfielder whose fitness regimen included three hundred pushups per week. He projected manliness and strength and his easy going, friendly nature people found impossible not to like. Even undesirable types saw he was *for* them, not out to nail them for anything he could. Women especially liked him.

It pleased Walker to see his prize pupil grasp District Six, the most diverse part of Bellevue, so well. The frontage road on the north side of the freeway held an eclectic collage of '50s vintage greasy spoons, fleabag no-tell motels, blue collar bars and taverns, a bowling alley, a steakhouse with live music, trailer parks, and a small private airport. Over the south city line, the lounge of the old Sunset Drive-in Theater, recently converted to a topless bar, the Bavarian Gardens, became the new hub of activity and revenue for massage parlors, prostitutes, pimps and straying husbands, all of whom sooner or later wandered into Eastgate.

Hitchcock routinely began his shift inspecting the industrial area located below the freeway. All but a few buildings would be closed by 8 PM. Tonight he and Walker moved building to building, in and out of their patrol car, leaving a window down so as to hear the radio in case a call came in.

Next they checked the bars along the north frontage road, starting at Charlie's Place, a neighborhood blue collar, pull-tab, pool table-and-beer joint known for fights. Truckers, mechanics, and construction workers, hung out there. Single women, (mostly divorced local moms) moonlighted there in the oldest profession on weekends to make ends meet. From Charlie's, it was a few yards' walk to two early '50s red brick motels renting rooms by the hour.

At Charlie's they parked at the edge of the back parking lot, shut off the motor, killed the lights, and sat in silence, the windows down a crack, watching, listening, absorbing and assessing. After an interminable silence, Walker grabbed the mike.

"Three Zero Six to Radio."

"Three Zero Six."

"We'll be out on a bar check at Charlie's."

"10-4. Three Zero Six out at Charlie's at 2109 Hours."

The half-dozen cars and pickups in the back lot indicated a slow night. But tomorrow - payday for most of the area businesses - would be busy. They adjusted their hats, slipped their batons into their belt rings and walked through the parking lot, probing inside parked cars with their flashlights; all were empty. At the rear door they paused a few seconds to assess the sounds inside before entering - country music, clinking pool balls and calm conversation prevailed. They drifted in, casual and friendly.

"Hey, Roger, how's it going?" greeted the owner, the mountainous Wallace Evans, a talkative, happy-go-lucky sort for whom having the bluesuits walk through every night made his bar a safer place; kept a lid on things. A family man who wanted people to call him Wally, Evans possessed a playful sense of humor and an endless repertoire of clean jokes. Tonight Hitchcock sensed something had Wally rattled.

"So, what's up, friend?"

"I was about to call you," Wally confided in a tone below the jukebox. "A strange guy left a minute ago. Had the look and way about him of having done hard time, a convict. Not only his appearance but his eyes and the way he moved creeped me out. In fact I'm still jumpy."

"Tell me more," Hitchcock urged.

Wally shook his head as he nervously wiped the bar with a rag. "Well, he did nothing wrong. Came in alone, ordered a beer, which he nursed at the corner table over there, and sat, watching me and my customers for about forty-minutes. Stone-faced, he was. I get strange people in here all the time, and I rarely worry. But this time—I can't put my finger on it, other than I think he was casing my place."

"Description?"

"White guy, maybe thirty-five, real pale skin, thin build, but appears to be very fit, maybe five-nine or ten, short brown hair, average features—but hard looking; hard eyes. Oh - he wore a medium blue shirt and a dark ski parka."

"Okay, any facial hair, scars, anything else? Did he say anything you remember?" Walker asked.

"No facial hair. He spoke only to order a beer when he came in. When I later asked if he wanted another, he shook his head no.

"I'm closing up at midnight and I'm asking you guys to be here when I close and follow me home—you know where I live."

"Sure. I'll tell the duty sergeant, so if we can't be here at midnight, another unit will."

The night clerks at the two motels next door hadn't seen anyone matching Wally's description. Because of the popularity of police scanners Hitchcock called Sergeant Breen from a pay phone to make his report and request a security detail off the air for Wally at closing.

Next they checked the Great Wall, a Chinese restaurant and lounge owned by Juju Kwan, a real looker from Taiwan in her early thirties, whose exotic beauty was rumored to be the ruin of several successful businessmen. Sandwiched between a tool rental shop and a mom and pop insurance agency in a 1950s vintage flat-roofed one-story brick building facing the north frontage road, The Great Wall opened daily for lunch and dinner, but after adjacent businesses closed, it drew rats, bats and alley cats; animal and human.

Hitchcock and Walker parked in the darkest part of the back lot and sat, engine and lights off, listening and watching. Except for the sounds of light traffic on the freeway, it was calm and quiet. They passed by Juju's shiny new Cadillac parked at the rear door as they strolled through the back door into the kitchen.

Hissing sounds came from several over-sized wok pans in which meat and vegetables sizzled, clouds of steam gushed upward, flying droplets of grease popped up and sideways from wok pans on stoves, a rush of pungent smells of Asian spices, seasonings and boiling rice greeted the officers' nostrils. At one food prep table, a squat, broad-faced Asian woman worked with a paring knife on four deer legs, hide and hooves intact, tossing chunks of tendon into a wok filled with raw vegetables. Chinese cooks barked orders to each other in their native tongue as they scurried around their work, ignoring the cops.

Hitchcock was astonished. *Deer legs? Wonder how they bill THAT on the menu! Wouldn't the Health Department just love to know about this!* He mused.

"Hi there, po-leese mans! Can I get you boys something? Some coffee, maybe, or tea? Tea I got." Juju came up alongside Hitchcock, wearing a sleeveless black dress. Her long black hair draped over her ivory shoulders like fine black silk, accentuating her sensual beauty. Brown almond-shaped eyes flashed invitingly up at him as she put a tiny hand on his arm, softly squeezing his bicep. Hitchcock didn't trust her. He had seen women like Juju running bars and brothels in Southeast Asia. Beneath the come-here-boy-me-like-you façade lurked a cruel, cunning tigress, eager to lure naive, sheltered men into falling for her, to their ruin.

In the short time Hitchcock had been assigned to Eastgate, he noticed Juju's employees consistently outnumbered the customers, which made profitability mathematically impossible. When he added Juju's new Cadillac, high-end jewelry and expensive wardrobe to her business overhead, the only reasonable conclusion is her restaurant and bar are fronts for drugs and other forms of vice.

Hitchcock resolved it would be a matter of time before he had enough on Juju to put her out of business; Juju resolved to either compromise Hitchcock by seducing him to protect her interests, or find another way to remove him as a threat.

"Nothing for us, thanks." Hitchcock said with a polite smile. "We're looking for a potentially dangerous man who may have come here tonight."

"Oh sure, Heetchcock. You go ahead, but you be careful please, *for me*, please, but what he look like?" Juju said, boldly looking at him, her hand still on his arm.

Walker repeated the description from Wally without mentioning the source. "No. No one come here like that," she promptly replied. They quickly scanned the bar crowd and left. Walker began laughing as soon as they got back in back in their car.

"What's so funny?"

"You—your face when we walked in," Walker said, still laughing. "Us older guys have been telling you and telling you, *never* eat at The Great Wall, but you never seemed to get it—until tonight—the surprise on your face when you saw deer legs next to the wok was priceless. And how quickly Juju moved in between you and the deer feet, placed her little hand on your arm and flashed those big browns at you, so you'd forget. And what happened? You forgot all about it! *Now* you get it!"

Always one to laugh at himself, Hitchcock laughed with Walker. "Yeah, Juju distracted me, all right. That's one on me. *Now* I get it!"

They checked the other bars: The Wagon Wheel—a western style restaurant and cocktail lounge, The Steak Out—a rowdy rock n' roll steakhouse and bar, and the Hilltop Inn—a two-story fleabag motel and cocktail lounge, well known for catering to drug dealers and hookers…no one had seen the man Wally described.

"I'd say ole Wally is getting a bit jumpy in his old age," Walker said meditatively.

Hitchcock was brooding. "I'm not so sure. Wally's been in the bar business too many years to not have good instincts," he said.

"Yeah, well, I'm hungry and its past ten so all the kitchens here are closed. Let's see if we can leave our district to eat."

"If you're hungry, the kitchen crew at the Great Wall will be glad to rustle up some deer leg for you. They'll have some left over by now. You know what that Euell Gibbons guy on TV always says: 'Many parts *are* edible.' How 'bout it?"

"Nah, they wouldn't have removed enough of the hair from the skin by now to suit my taste. Sambo's is safer—all I'll need there is a roll of Tums, not an ambulance," Walker chuckled as he reached for the mike.

"Three Zero Six to radio."

"Radio to Three Zero Six, go," came the reply.

"Request permission to leave our district to 10-34 at Sambo's."

"Permission granted, Three Zero Six."

Hitchcock headed toward the freeway. Radio called back.

"All units standby. Three Zero Six, return to your district. Three Zero Eight, start moving toward District Six to back up Three Zero Six. All units stand by: emergency traffic only."

Hitchcock pulled into an empty parking lot and waited. The silence was heavy. The mounting tension reminded Hitchcock of hearing a distant shot in the jungle and waiting to see if the bullet finds you. To do something, anything, Walker lit a cigarette. And they waited.

"Radio to Three Zero Six, Three Zero Eight, respond Code Three to a fight-in-progress with one man unconscious from head injuries at the Ridge Apartments at 2931 145th Avenue SE. We have an ambulance on the way. The scene is an unknown apartment on the second floor. We are on the phone with a second injured victim, getting more details."

Hitchcock had been to the complex. It was located right outside the entrance to the new community college campus. He flipped the console switch for the overhead red light and shifted into drive.

"Three Zero Six en route," Walker replied.

"Radio to responding units: victim on the phone says the suspect is a Bob Sandoval, white male, mid-twenties, thin build, taking cocaine and alcohol, said he is going to commit suicide with his car and take someone with him. Injured roommate tried to keep the keys from him and the suspect struck him on the head with a brick. Suspect has fled the apartment. His vehicle is a new, white Triumph TR-6 sports car, unknown license."

Seconds later the radio buzzed. "Three Zero Eight, Radio, 10-97 at the Ridge Apartments. A white TR6 is leaving the parking lot; Washington plate Adam Queen Boy Seven Two Six. Heading northbound on 148th. He is not stopping."

"Allard's on him and they're headed our way." Hitchcock turned right onto southbound 145th Avenue and accelerated hard, fast approaching the rear of a stationwagon. Hitchcock flipped the siren switch and hit the horn ring. *Aaaaahhhh,uuuhhhh,aahhhh* it whined.

"Pull over, dammit!" Walker shouted, bracing his feet against the floor and his left hand on the wood stock of the shotgun as the distance rapidly closed. Instead of pulling over, the stationwagon stopped in the southbound lane. With only a foot to spare, Hitchcock hit the siren again and swerved into the oncoming lane, whizzing past the wagon.

"Three Zero Eight, radio. Suspect turning left on SE 22nd street, heading to 145th."

"Three Zero Six is already on 145th, and we see you, Three Zero Eight."

Hitchcock and Allard—another Vietnam vet—hotly pursued the TR6 up and down a grid of intersecting two-lane residential streets and four-lane avenues, clocking speeds of 60, 70, even 80 miles per hour. Allard tried to ram the TR6 when it spun out trying to make a ninety degree right turn at an intersection. It escaped by an inch and roared southbound toward the freeway, resuming higher speeds.

Again Dispatch broke in: "Radio to Three Zero Six and Three Zero Eight, Records confirms suspect Sandoval has an outstanding felony warrant for assault first degree, attempted murder out of Pierce County and another for escape. Consider armed and dangerous."

Past the college entrance at SE 24th, southbound 148th Avenue drops bumpily straight downhill to a T-intersection at the westbound freeway lanes, making a hard right turn onto the north frontage road the only option. At the last possible moment, the TR6 brake lights came on as it turned violently to the right. Sparks flew like an armload of Fourth of July sparklers as it careened off the concrete barrier between the road end and the freeway, and accelerated west with Allard and Hitchcock right behind, unshakable — albeit with less agile cars — lights and sirens in full effect.

The TR6 roared past Charlie's and Cane's Motel, took the short onramp onto the westbound freeway and accelerated downhill. Allard overran the onramp and tried to leap the ditch onto the freeway at seventy, collapsing the left front wheel when it struck the ditch shoulder. He was out of the chase. Hitchcock shot across the ramp at over seventy, now the lead pursuit car.

Allard keyed his radio mike: "Three Zero Eight, Radio, my vehicle is out of commission on the frontage road in front of The Great Wall. Will need a tow truck. Three Zero Six is continuing pursuit westbound I-90."

"Received. Three Zero Eight is disabled, Three Zero Six still in pursuit, westbound I-90."

Hitchcock punched the pedal. Quickly the gap began closing. Walker stared straight ahead, mute, transfixed, his left hand gripping the wood stock of the shotgun as if he would squeeze blood from it. It began to rain. Fear crept into Hitchcock. The wipers barely shuddered across the windshield, the wind was so strong

Another voice came on the air."Three Zero Five in position to assist Three Zero Six in the pursuit at I-90 and Bellevue Way, Radio."

"Good! That's Sherman, he's a former race driver," Walker announced with confidence.

Yet another voice came on the air. "Three Zero Six, this is Four-Twenty, Sergeant Breen. What is your speed now?"

Walker glanced at the dash. "Uh, like a hundred twenty, maybe, Sarge," he gulped.

A long pause followed as the speed sank in to everyone's minds.

"Alright—call it off," Breen finally ordered.

Hitchcock dared not take his eyes off the road. By now his field of vision had narrowed in concert with increasing speed to the point that the road ahead became an ever-tightening tunnel in which TR6 taillights were all he saw ahead. It crossed his mind that at this speed his cruiser was not in contact with the pavement; only water, underscored by the almost total lightness he felt in the steering wheel. To take his eyes off the road for even a split-second meant instant death. He was gaining on the TR6 fast and now Tom Sherman was in the rearview mirror, overhead light flashing, gaining fast.

"Again, this is Sergeant Breen calling Three Zero Six. You are ordered to break off the pursuit. Now. Can you hear?"

In seconds they would be crossing the East Channel Bridge out of Bellevue to Mercer Island. Walker glanced at Hitchcock.

"Aw Hell!" Walker turned the radio off.

Sergeant Breen paced nonstop in the dispatch room, listening, chain smoking, sweating. He knew from the silence the chase was still on. A thousand "what if's" raced through his mind. He snapped his fingers at the assisting dispatcher.

"Polly! Quick! Call Seattle PD Dispatch. Tell them we have two units chasing an escaped felon on I-90. They're crossing Mercer Island at high speed and headed their way." Polly placed the call. Seattle Police units from the Capitol Hill Precinct were dispatched to take up positions above the freeway to intercept the chase.

Hitchcock's cruiser began fishtailing on the wet pavement of the East Channel Bridge. Cold fear seeped into his limbs, taking him to the edge of paralysis. Heart pounding in his throat, he steeled himself, focusing on holding the wheel steady and letting off the accelerator rather than trying to counter the swaying. The big black-and-white quickly resumed steady in-line travel and a relieved Hitchcock re-applied acceleration. The nimble TR6 could outmaneuver, but on the straightaway the Fury was king. The gap began closing. Hitchcock hoped for a chance to disable the TR6 by either ramming or shooting it before it reached Seattle where someone would be killed.

The TR6 crossed the bridge at over a hundred, went up the first off-ramp on Mercer Island and became airborne past the stop sign at the crest. A sedan was crossing the overpass toward the off-ramp as Hitchcock also flew up the ramp and went airborne by about three feet. The TR6 landed on the gravel shoulder in a crash, engine stalled. Seeing the danger of the pursuit in progress, the sedan on the overpass braked hard and went into a slide on the wet pavement as Hitchcock sailed through the air, narrowly missing a fatal accident. Hitchcock felt the steering wheel loosen. To avoid landing with the wheels turned, he held it straight by stiffening his arms. He glanced down, making eye contact with the driver of the sedan as he sailed by. The cruiser landed in a nose-first, two-part crash onto the shoulder in an exploding hail of dirt and gravel, stalling the engine as the TR6 roared to life and disappeared around the bend in the freeway. Sherman's cruiser flashed by them, taking over the chase.

Hitchcock restarted his engine and rejoined the chase as Sherman rounded the bend in time to see the close-set taillights zip down the next off-ramp and disappear. Downshifting, Sherman found the TR6 spun out while taking a hard left under the freeway, stalled, facing him. Two Mercer Island patrol cars arrived, lights flashing, blocking escape to the rear. Sherman approached calmly, shotgun at the shoulder, aiming through the windshield at the driver, who tried desperately to restart the engine. When the suspect looked at him Sherman racked a round into the chamber and flicked the safety off.

"You're under arrest! Put your hands on the dash, palms up!"

"Get ready to die with me, pig!" Sandoval screamed, his face deathly white and contorted with rage. Flipping Sherman his middle finger, he turned the ignition again. The motor whirred but failed to turn over. The two Mercer Island officers approached, guns drawn, as Hitchcock and Walker ran up. Walker jerked on the driver door—locked. Sandoval, shaking his head and screaming obscenities, turned the key again; this time it sounded like it would start. Sherman pointed his shotgun at the hood of the TR6, finger on the trigger

"Hold your fire!" Hitchcock yelled. He swung the head of his heavy flashlight completely through the driver-door window, showering Sandoval with broken safety glass. Walker's mighty arms reached in, and in one smooth motion Sandoval was lifted by the front of his jacket through the window as if he were no more than a wet towel. Walker effortlessly body-slammed him face-down on the pavement, arms and legs flailing in futile resistance. Hitchcock quickly cuffed his hands behind him. Both officers jerked him upright and half-carried him to the back of their patrol car and belted him in.

Walker turned the radio back on and keyed the mike: "Three Zero Six, radio: we're en route to Overlake E.R. with one in custody. Three Zero Five will stand by to impound the car from Mercer Island."

Walker's report was drowned out by Sandoval's shouts and kicking the doors and the roof. "Pull over, Roger. We gotta stop him—he's kicking the windows now—he'll break the glass if we don't."

Sandoval kicked, spit, and cursed the officers as they fought him out of the car onto the pavement, removed his shoes, cuffed his feet together and applied a third set of cuffs to connect his feet to his hands behind his back. They set him face-down on the back seat. For the rest of the trip to the hospital Sandoval was subdued, grunting to Walker's efforts to keep him conscious with questions

.

Two orderlies with a gurney and a uniformed security guard waited outside the emergency entrance when they arrived. Sandoval sang softly to himself as Walker helped load him face down onto the gurney and wheeled him into the crowded emergency room.

"Isn't that awfully uncomfortable for the young man?" demanded a bespectacled, slender young doctor, his bearded jaw jutting forth with contempt.

Walker tried to explain. "Well, you see, Doc, he assaulted this guy tonight, and fled when we ..."

"That doesn't give you the right to truss him up like a wild animal. Set him loose, officer!"

"But, Doc, he's ..." Walker pleaded.

The doc's face flushed red with anger, blue veins stood out on his forehead "Officer, I DEMAND you remove the handcuffs from this poor young man AT ONCE!" he shouted, waving his arms in the air.

"With all due respect, this man is dangerous, Doc. He's an escaped felon, and as of tonight he's facing multiple felony assault charges, so no matter what, he's going with us. We'll wait on the other side of the curtain."

"Good! Now out-out-out!" the doctor quipped, pointing toward the curtain.

Hitchcock got on the phone with Sergeant Breen while Walker chatted with the hospital security officer. A woman's scream pierced the air, followed by sounds of crashing and breaking glass. Hitchcock exchanged glances with Walker, grinned and knowingly shook his head.

The nurse who had been with the doctor rushed out, hair disheveled, her white uniform askew. "Officers, help! He's attacking Doctor Philips and I can't stop him!"

"Sarge, I gotta go. The prisoner's attacking the doctor," Hitchcock told Sergeant Breen.

"Take him to Harborview, Roger," Breen ordered.

Hitchcock and Walker charged through the white curtains to the rescue of Dr. Philips, whom Sandoval was dragging across the floor through a puddle of liquid chemicals and broken glass. As Hitchcock broke Sandoval's grip on Doctor Phillips, and Walker powered him to the floor, an over-zealous security guard stepped in and over-sprayed Sandoval's face with chemical mace, immediately incapacitating everyone.

Amid outbursts of anger, burning eyes and gasping for breath, Hitchcock and Walker managed to fight through the chemical and restrain Sandoval again.

"Get that animal out of here! Take him to Harborview!" a trembling, terrified Doctor Phillips shrieked.

Even with the fan at full force and the windows down as they traveled the freeway, the mace was unbearable. Twice they stopped on the shoulder and got out for air as Sandoval hummed and sang unintelligibly. On the elevator ride to the ninth floor psych ward, Sandoval tried to bite Walker's hand. For Walker, who came in for a quiet ride with Hitchcock to escape his troubles for a night, enough was enough.

So the orderly wouldn't see it, Walker gently laid his right hand on Sandoval's arm and covered it with his left as he pinched and twisted hunks of skin, while soothingly asking "Oh, poor Bob! Is everything all right now, Bob? You'll be fine here, Bob. You'll like it here, Bob." Sandoval grunted "Uhhh!" with each pinch. Reaching the ninth floor, they helped orderlies fight Sandoval into a padded cell before returning to Bellevue. It was one-thirty.

Sambo's was dead except for one customer. Hitchcock ordered ham and eggs over easy; no hash browns or toast. For Walker it was a burger and fries. Both had coffee. They topped off their meal with a smoke in silence, numbed by the night's adrenalin-charged events.

Sergeant Breen flashed his spotlight at them as they left Sambo's. They pulled up alongside Breen, windows down.

"You ought to be the first to know," Breen told them, "the first victim in the apartment was pronounced dead a half hour ago at the county hospital and the second victim, the one who called us, is in critical condition and is not expected to live. So, you guys were chasing a murderer."

Breen paused, looking out his windshield. "Gotta say it—
good thing your radio "failed" and you didn't let him go—
somebody else would surely have died. Detectives will want
your reports when you come back tonight. Finish the shift,
get some rest. Somebody will complain, so before they do,
I'll be writing up commendations for you boys."

With that, Sergeant Jack Breen, always the cops' cop, drove
off.

In silence they rechecked the industrial district as the last
mission of the shift. As Hitchcock refueled after he dropped
Walker off at his car, it seemed to him as if an unseen Hand
had reached down and restored things to normal. Another
unit had escorted Wally Evans home from Charlie's at
midnight. At the city gas pumps, Hitchcock checked his
cruiser. Even after all they had put it through, it was
undamaged. He remembered a comment by a sergeant:
"Plymouth builds a cheap, tough car."

As Hitchcock gathered his gear at the end of shift, something
caught his eye. *What's this?* He looked closer—the outline of
a hand on the shotgun shoulder stock. *Is it grease?* He felt it
with his hand—*Oho!* It was Walker's handprint, pressed
right into the wood!

2

HITCHCOCK

The sloshing of his waterbed awakened him from a fitful sleep. Hitchcock's eyes squinted, seeking the clock on his nightstand. It was past noon; morning for him. He felt drained from the adrenalin rush of the night before. Over a steaming mug of yesterday's coffee he mused on how last night's death and violence represented the new America he had come home to. This isn't the America he grew up in; the America he grew up in would never call servicemen 'baby killers' or policemen 'pigs.' America became a nation of snide scofflaws while he was away, plagued with rising violent crime, social discord, disillusionment and drug addiction.

He wondered what the celebrities and news media people who publicly glorified drugs would have to say about last night: a man is dead, another would probably die, yet another would be returning to prison, and several others, himself included, and barely escaped death. None of it would have happened if not for the influence of drugs. He also noted how everyone involved were of his baby-boom generation.

A short four years earlier, narcotics were pretty much confined to Asian opium dens and the fringe elements of the big cities. Love of country was strong—desecrating the flag or scorning military service was unthinkable. Everything is upside down now. Veterans are vicious baby killers, policemen are pigs; right is wrong—wrong is right. Ordinary crime is politicized; the weakest excuses for criminal behavior are blithely accepted in the courts. Even Bellevue, Hitchcock's hometown, formerly a quiet place nicknamed "Seattle's bedroom," did not escape the windstorm of change.

Back-to-back annexations during the late 60s tripled Bellevue's territory as well as its population while Hitchcock was in 'Nam, transforming it from a sleepy upper-middle-class suburban Mayberry to Washington's fourth largest city. The new diversity brought growing pains as the new city limits stretched from Lake Washington to Lake Sammamish, encompassing what Bellevue had never known before: blue-collar neighborhoods, light manufacturing, high-density low income apartments, trailer parks, massage parlors and topless bars.

Big city problems came with it. Few people recognized the police force now faced the brunt of "real" crime on a regular basis; it wasn't mostly traffic and shoplifters any more. The citizenry and city administration had yet to grasp the scope of permanent changes that the annexations brought. In spite of its new status as a real city, Bellevue would never shed its original but unfair hoity-toity image.

Bellevue's struggle to change with the growth was uneven and colorful: Overlake Hospital, now four years old, opened an emergency room; the first one east of Seattle, earlier in 1970, but no one seemed to notice the city lacked an ambulance service. Instead, Bellevue contracted with Flintoff's Mortuary in Issaquah, ten miles away, to transport the injured in their hearses, giving rise to officers' humorous speculations about what the injured must think when they wake up in a hearse.

Hitchcock served two one-year tours as an Army medic in Vietnam. He shocked his family by enlisting for three years, choosing to step away from his college draft deferment.

Breaking ranks and standing apart yet being a team player was in character for Hitchcock: as a teen he dismayed his family by excelling in competitive boxing as his father had in his youth. He chose to earn his own money working summertime jobs in heavy construction, road repair and in a local slaughterhouse even though as a doctor's son, he didn't have to. Even as a boy, Roger Hitchcock was the family maverick who modeled himself after his father but marched to a different drummer. He was a veteran who found his calling as a cop now, not a pre-med student, and he loved it.

Downing the last swig of reheated coffee, Hitchcock slipped into a pair of well-worn blue jeans, buttoned and tucked in his favorite shirt—navy blue wool, washed and worn to the point of baby-blanket softness—and old penny-loafers. He checked and belted on his holstered off-duty .38 Smith & Wesson snubnose, covered it with a black windbreaker. Taking his gym bag, he stepped outside. He felt the crisp edge of autumn as he fired up his two-tone gold '64 El Camino to get to the Pancake Corral before they closed at two.

"What'll you have, Roger—the usual?"

"Coffee, Ada, and the Weightlifter's Special, medium rare."

Hitchcock had been coming to the Pancake Corral most of his life. His father brought him there often, even before Bill Chace bought it when it was Nick's BBQ, locally famous for "ham hamburgers." Located well south of the downtown core, the Pancake Corral is an icon of Old Bellevue, a mom-and-pop American diner, the kind that never changes. Bill Chace and his wife, Lois, were working owners, and daughters Ada and Jane had spent much of their youth waitressing and learning the business.

The Corral was empty and ready to close when Hitchcock headed to the register. The ever-cheerful Bill Chace, tall and still athletic into his late fifties, came up to ring him out.

"Hitch, you're looking more like your dad all the time—you're even built like he was. Ted was one of my best friends, and the most gifted doctor I ever knew. His passing was a terrible loss to all of us. God rest his soul," said Bill reverently. Hitchcock smiled and started to leave.

"Oh!" said Bill with a snap of his fingers. "Almost forgot— one of the gals who works here wants to talk to you about something, Hitch," said Bill—who liked to invent nicknames for his favorite customers.

"Who and what?" inquired Hitchcock, noticing Bill's sly grin as he casually put a toothpick between his teeth.

"It's the one you have your eye on every time you're here."

"Oh? And which one would that be?" Hitchcock inquired with a sheepish smirk.

"Oh come on, Hitch!" Bill laughed. "It's Allie, the good looking little blond; says its important and wants you to call her as soon as you can. She's off today. Said to give you her number if you came in," Bill said, handing him a piece of note paper.

"Is this business or personal?"

Bill smiled and shrugged. "Guess you'll have to find out," he winked as he headed to the back, thinking *Oh to be young again.*

He dropped a dime into the pay phone in the waiting area and dialed. He recognized Allie's voice when she answered.

"Hi Roger, thanks for calling me. I have information for you in case something happens to me. I won't say what it is on the phone. I have my son with me until my ex picks him up about two hours from now. Can you meet me after that? It's important, very important."

Allison Malloy lived in a small apartment on the southwest edge of downtown Bellevue. They agreed to meet in a bank parking lot a block from her apartment in three hours. Hitchcock went to the gym and worked his Wednesday routine, warming up with light calisthenics, punching a heavy bag, skipping rope, a hundred pushups in four sets of twenty-five reps, followed by light weightlifting, ending with full-length pull-ups to the point of failure. He finished and showered in an hour-and-a-half. At Nick's on Park Row, near where he would meet Allie, he treated himself to a green salad and a large hunk of grilled beef brisket.

Bank employees were leaving when Hitchcock parked at the far edge of the parking lot. He wondered what this was about. Other than casual chit-chat at the Corral, he didn't know Allie, though he couldn't help admiring her; a natural blonde, beautiful, and pleasant.

She arrived ten minutes early in a tired gray Toyota sedan with worn tires. She parked next to his El Camino and walked up to his passenger side. He had never seen Allie away from work before. He liked what he saw. Five-foot-one, shapely and petite, somewhere in her early twenties, her raw femininity was radioactive through her loose-fitting khakis and blue baggy man's sweatshirt with paint stains, and unkempt neck-length golden hair. Obviously her intentions in seeing him weren't social. She was dressed in grubbies, which allowed him to see the depth of her beauty without makeup, and her lack of pretentiousness in meeting him this way. Hitchcock had never been so impressed. He opened the door for her from inside. She got right to the point as she got in.

"Thanks for meeting me, Roger. My ex is at my place with my son. I have only a few minutes," Allie began with penetrating eye contact, "so I'll be quick about it. I'm telling you about this because you are the only cop I know and everyone at work speaks well of you. There is this strange guy who I think is dangerous. I've only met with him briefly twice but he keeps calling me at night and he talks a lot of angry political stuff. He keeps trying to get me to see things from his point of view."

"Like…?"

"He says poor working people like me have no chance at all because we're being exploited by the rich, who are protected by the police; the whole system is rigged and needs to be changed, with violence. I'm not into politics so I don't have much to say in response, which he must be interpreting as agreement, so he thinks I'm a candidate for his group."

"Group? What group?"

"Not sure. But whatever it is, he says it's armed with guns and its intentions are violent. Last week on my day off I agreed to meet him for coffee at Ramona's Café in North Towne. He showed me his pistol and told me the group he's part of is forming for some kind of war. He had a military term for it, but I can't remember it." Allie paused.

"Roger, this guy is so intense it's scary. He's trying to recruit me. He's told me so much I'm afraid of what will happen if I cut him off from calling. I have an infant son, so I don't date. I only met this guy a couple times because I felt sorry for him—he seemed lonely and harmless. But all he does is talk politics; radical, far-out stuff like robbing banks and liquor stores to buy weapons. I am telling you this in case something happens to me. He says his name is Jim Randall, which I doubt is real, and here's his phone number—I've never called it so I don't know if it's any good."

After giving Hitchcock a physical description of Randall, his car, and other details, Allie left. Without her knowing it he tailed her to see if she was being followed. He parked across the street and studied her climbing the stairs to her second-floor apartment. *Even her going upstairs is somehow feminine,* he thought.

He waited to see what her ex-husband is like. Within a few seconds a nondescript, diminutive man with dirty, shoulder-length mouse-brown hair, appearing to be in his early thirties, stepped out of Allie's apartment. Though shabbily dressed in a worn ski parka and jeans, his bearing had an air of snooty superiority. To Hitchcock's surprise, instead of a VW bus or some other hippy-rig, he drove away in a shiny red late model Mercedes sedan so obviously inconsistent with his appearance and with Allie's grim financial status it puzzled Hitchcock. *There's serious money here,* he speculated. He followed the Mercedes long enough to note the plate number before heading to his apartment to prepare for work.

On his way home he assessed his desire to protect Allie but brushed it off as merely typical of his upbringing. His father instilled in him a strong instinct to protect the weak. The sudden death of his father, followed by experiencing life on the edge in a hot war zone, where there was dying and suffering all around him forged in him a different life view and values than he had before the war and strengthened his protective instincts toward the weak and vulnerable..

Much of what he took so seriously before the Army he disdained as superfluous. He saw life now as short, fragile, tenuous, and cheap; death can come any time to anyone. Humanity is divided into in two categories: sheep and wolves. Most people are sheep; easily herded, easily fooled, easily distracted, helpless. There are two subclasses of wolves: predators and protectors. Hitchcock recognized a seemingly divine balance in the equation: citizens are sheep, prey for the predators; cops and soldiers are society's protectors— predators under authority for whom society's predators are *their* prey.

And besides, Allie is divorced and has a child. A ready-made family he didn't need.

Competitive boxing and Army life taught him that discipline and readiness to fight are the keys to survival, and in exercising these Hitchcock remained diligent. In addition to physical fitness he made it his custom before going to work to empty his service revolver and practice twenty-five draws from the holster, aiming at a piece of paper taped to the bedroom door at chest level. Slowly at first; speed accumulated naturally until he had reached the desired number of draws and level of speed. The goal being to develop muscle memory to enable his body to fight instinctively fight on its own in a crisis.

Wednesday, 7:45 p.m. Sergeant Breen stood behind the podium as the men of Third Shift sat down for briefing.

"The news-hounds are all over the story of last night's homicide and the pursuit that led to the suspect's arrest. If anyone, news media or not, asks you, do *not* comment. Refer them to Captain Whittington, our press information officer." Breen continued. "Also, although the chief is fielding questions and complaints about our pursuit of Sandoval last night, from me, I want to say 'well done' to those of you who kept this guy from escaping. It's a miracle no one else got killed or injured. Detectives filed murder and assault charges on Sandoval today and he is being held on other state charges as well.

"I want Hitchcock, Allard, and Sherman to get your reports from last night written up as soon as possible. Should be quiet tonight. I'll pick them up in the field. Disssmissed!"

District assignments were announced. Walker was back on duty and working in District Eight next to Hitchcock, and Hitchcock's gut instinct was acting up again.

3

PRIMAL INSTINCTS

In 'Nam, Hitchcock learned to trust his gut. Tonight, his gut told him to change his routine and be at Charlie's. After shift briefing he approached Walker in the station parking lot.

"Let's meet at the back of Charlie's right now, radio silence," he said. It was Wednesday, Friday for Hitchcock and Monday for Walker.

"Something's up?" asked Walker.

"Yeah. Something tells me we should go there first."

"Okay. See you in the back of the lot."

A soft drizzle dampened the mood of the night. Radio traffic was light. As it was the 20th, the last payday of the month, it would be busy at Charlie's. Nearly two dozen cars and pickups were in the rear and front lots, all unoccupied. As they approached the rear door, a young bearded man in a red plaid shirt and dark knit cap stepped out the back door. He stopped cold when he saw the officers and rushed back inside.

As one man they ran to the rear door. Hitchcock slid in first. Wally busily wiped the bar with a damp rag, making a show of pretending he didn't see Hitchcock, whose eyes searched for the red plaid shirt. The place was packed. Several construction workers in rough canvas coats, overalls and ball caps huddled around a corner table, nursing their beers. The man in the red plaid shirt hadn't time to go out the front door. Debbie, the blonde barmaid, a pretty and friendly girl, glanced nervously at the officers without her usual greeting. Hitchcock took this as a trouble signal. He discreetly nudged the butt of his revolver with his elbow to locate its exact location on his hip as he scanned the darkest corners. No red shirt. Walker blocked the rear door, thumbs hooked into his gun belt, eyes on his partner, the customers, and the front door.

Wally continued wiping the bar without looking up. "What can I do for you, *officer*?" Wally's greeting Hitchcock by his title was the second trouble signal: he and Wally were on a first-name basis.

"How are things tonight, *bartender*?" Hitchcock asked, acknowledging Wally's coded warning, staring hard at the big man.

"Oh, you know, it's another quiet Wednesday," Wally said, motioning leftward with his eyes to the women's restroom located next to the rear door. "You know how it always is on nights like these, *officer* ..." his voice trailing off.

"Very well, bartender. Have a good evening," Hitchcock nodded acknowledgement as he turned toward the women's restroom, drawing his revolver. With a "cover me" nod to Walker he tried the women's room door. It was being blocked from the inside. He knocked. No response.

"Police! I know you're in there! Come out now." No answer.

Hitchcock pushed hard on the door. Someone inside was leaning against it. He put his shoulder against the door and leaned into it. The door gave way; into the closet-sized restroom he went, gun first. "Don't shoot, officer, I'm clean," announced a man, his voice a calm, deadly hiss. He was small and wiry, clean-shaven, a ferret in human form.

"Get your hands up, no funny business."

Reptilian eyes coldly assessed Hitchcock as the man's hands smoothly ascended. His features bore witness to what he was: small, but deadly quick, a cold life-taker. The space was too tight to turn and frisk him without risk of a struggle for his gun. Hitchcock's left hand grabbed the front of the ferret's shirt as his right hand pressed the barrel of his revolver under his chin. The suspect's eyes widened with fear when Hitchcock, staring straight into him, cocked the hammer.

"Now … we're going out of here together, like this, in small steps. Keep your hands up, without fail," Hitchcock ordered in a low voice as he walked slowly backward, finger on the trigger, pulling the suspect step-by-step with him out of the restroom, each man staring intently at the other. Hitchcock saw in the man's eyes a cornered predator, cold lethality like he had not seen since Vietnam. The predator recognized in Hitchcock a protector experienced in life-taking in the course of duty, who understood the upper hand was his, and would not hesitate to kill to keep it. It was either comply or die on the spot.

The bar crowd was on its feet, stone silent as Hitchcock and his prisoner inched their way into the open. He holstered his weapon as Walker cuffed the suspect and patted him down, finding a thin, flat, long-bladed knife—the prison-made kind—scotch-taped to his bare chest under a blue button-front work shirt; the hilt at the solar plexus for quick access with either hand. Nothing in his pockets, not even a wallet.

"Who are you and what's going on here?" Walker demanded. The man said nothing. Hitchcock left the suspect with Walker and returned to the restroom. In the waste basket, hidden under a pile of paper towels, he found a red plaid flannel shirt, a knit cap, fake beard, a man's wallet, a car key and at the bottom he found a loaded 9mm Browning Hi-Power pistol, its magazine fully loaded with thirteen rounds. Hitchcock returned, keeping the seized pistol out of view. He held the beard, cap and shirt up to the suspect's face.

"Start talking," he demanded.

The suspect calmly lowered his head and looked away, saying nothing. Only experienced criminals are this cool. Hitchcock wondered if he and Walker inadvertently averted a mass armed robbery or murder by walking in when they did. Walker took him to the patrol car and waited while Hitchcock obtained the names of all the customers inside and talked with Wally.

Wally was white-faced and shaking. "*This* is the guy I told you about last night! Same guy! *Now* he comes in wearing this disguise, starts to go out the back, and hides in the women's room when he sees you two."

"What did he do tonight, Wally?"

"He came about an hour ago, and sat alone in the corner over there. Had one beer, just like before; drinking and watching the customers, not saying a word, looking all around. Seconds before you arrived he went to the front door. I thought he was going to leave but he didn't. He went to the back door, and suddenly ran back in and ducked into the women's restroom. I had *no idea* it was the same guy — I had a bad feeling when he came in, real bad. Now this …," Wally gestured to the wig, fake beard and change of clothing.

Someone outside began pounding on the front door. "Hey, open up! You can't be closed this early!" shouted a male voice outside.

Wally rushed to the door "What the -? It's locked! Someone locked my front door from the inside!"

Two male regulars came through, but Wally sent them away; he was done for the night. Hitchcock used the phone behind the bar to call Sergeant Breen as Wally sent his customers away.

In the patrol car, the suspect argued with Walker. "You got nothing to hold me for, officer, better let me go or you'll be hearing from my attorney in the morning."

"You're not going anywhere. You had a knife hidden on your body, you attempted to hide from us in the bar, you have no ID and you refuse to identify yourself. So if you want to be freed, identifying yourself would be a good place to start."

"There's no crime here, no proof I've done anything I could legally be held for, so let me go, please," the suspect persisted.

Hitchcock came out, carrying the evidence in two paper bags, which he placed in the trunk of his cruiser. When Walker apprised him of the situation, Hitchcock roughly pulled the suspect out.

"Here's how it is. I'm arresting you for unlawful carrying of a concealed weapon. Now, who are you and how did you get here?"

The suspect, twisting his wrists within the handcuffs behind him, shook his head, laughing in Hitchcock's face. "The gun wasn't on me, officer, you got nothing, and if you got nothing, I don't have to tell you who I am," he announced with confidence.

"Well, well! *Who* said there is a gun? *You* did! The gun is yours, by your own words. Thank you much," said Hitchcock in a tone of mock cheer.

The suspect looked away, grim-faced at his mistake, shifting his wrists within the handcuffs. Hitchcock tried taunting him into talking more. "I wasn't referring to the gun anyway —it's the knife."

"Not illegal in Washington! You ought to know," he retorted, spitting his words.

"In *my* district it is. I'm betting we'll find your prints on the gun and the front door latch, where you intended to hold everybody hostage and rob each one at gunpoint. You're probably wanted somewhere too, from the look of you."

"No more talk. I want an attorney," he said resignedly.

Hitchcock conferred with Sergeant Breen when he arrived. The parking lot was empty except for one car by the time Hitchcock finished taking detailed written statements from Wally and Debbie. The key found with the gun and the disguise fit the car, a well-maintained white, late '60s Pontiac sedan registered to a Harper Wilcox, address across the state in Yakima. Records contacted the owner by phone to learn he loaned the car to his nephew, Colin, who had been paroled from the state pen at Walla Walla six months ago. Hitchcock called for an impound truck and inventoried the contents. In the glove box he found what he expected: a partly empty carton of brand-name 9mm ammunition and another loaded magazine.

Under both sides of the front seat were cash receipts and matchbooks from various bars, restaurants and motels. What he found next stopped him cold—two receipts and a matchbook from The Great Wall. One receipt was from last night, time-stamped only an hour before he and Walker stopped by and talked to Juju—the other receipt had been time-stamped *an hour ago.*

4
CODES OF HONOR

Hitchcock sealed the doors and windows of the Pontiac with evidence tape. He told the tow truck driver to keep it secured and sealed for the detectives. He expected to find ammunition and a loaded second magazine linking the suspect to the gun in the women's restroom, but the receipts from The Great Wall added a new twist—Wilcox was there twice in the past week; the last time just an hour before his arrest at Charlie's. Coincidence? In his gut Hitchcock knew better. It was impossible Juju didn't see him; both nights were quiet and Juju always greeted male customers, especially if they were alone. *She lied to me, and I need to know why*, he thought.

For a woman of Juju's financial status to be connected with an armed criminal wearing disguises and lurking about in local businesses at night, suggested something bad was up. Hitchcock suspected the Pontiac held more than evidence of illegal firearm possession. The next step would be to get a search warrant for the car, a job for detectives

Even during booking the suspect refused to identify himself. By the time he was placed in a holding cell, reports were written, evidence was labeled and packaged, Records notified Hitchcock confirmed his suspect is Colin Wilcox, age thirty-seven, wanted by the state Department of

Corrections for parole violation. He had been paroled seven months ago after serving three years of a ten-year sentence for murder that was reduced to manslaughter in Yakima County. His rap sheet included multiple arrests for burglary and armed robbery in rural Yakima, Chelan and Spokane counties, most of which were negotiated away. It struck Hitchcock as odd that Wilcox, a reputed professional hit man, had no known history of being in Western Washington, yet he came to the Seattle area almost as soon as he was paroled. Why? After writing up notes for the detective division, Hitchcock went home to some time off.

* * *

The end of September was fast approaching when a young frizzy-haired hippy chick from upstairs knocked on his door. She seemed nervous when he opened it.

"Hey Roger-man, I'm Willow, your upstairs neighbor, and I think you're kinda cool and macho, and uh, well, I want to give you Ollie, my pet rock. You know, it's a friendship gift, so your rock and my rock, Fawn, could date, OK?"

Hitchcock stared at Willow—pretty, but scrawny and pale, with wildly frizzy light brown hair, holding a flat stone painted lime green with a face, in her hand. Dumbfounded, he could only reply, "Huh?"

"Yeah, see, my rock is a girl and needs a guy, and Ollie is going to miss his rock-woman, so, maybe we could get them together for a date with Fawn at my place upstairs, say Saturday night?"

Hitchcock smiled kindly at her. "Maybe next month, Willow. I'll have to take a rain check. You see, I'm working nights right now, including Saturdays. Thanks, though, for giving me Ollie — this is thoughtful of you."

Right away Hitchcock notified the manager he was leaving. He hadn't found a new place yet, but he had had it with apartment living. Pressed for time, he searched all day for a house or cabin to rent, but found none suitable.

Thursdays were the only day the Corral was open for dinner, set to serve one dish only — Lois' locally famous homemade New England style chili and cornbread. Hitchcock, who loved simple grub, stopped by, not only to eat, but to check on Allie, whose schedule he knew well.

As luck would have it, who was there when he strolled in but Doc Henderson and his wife Ethel. When Hitchcock saw the retired veterinarian, fond childhood memories of his father returned. Dad took the young Roger to Doc's clinic to pick out his first dog, where he selected a golden Collie like the one in the Lassie movies, and named him Champ.

Hitchcock accepted Doc's invitation to sit with them, and Allie took over as their waitress as they caught up on family news. As he knew they would, Doc and Ethel reminisced about his father. When he mentioned his housing dilemma,

Doc and Ethel immediately offered their cabana. "The state trooper who lived there moved out. Come see it – it has a fireplace, kitchen, full bath, all you need," Doc said.

The setting was ideal for the country boy in Hitchcock. A long, tree-lined, single-lane gravel road led like a journey back in time to the Henderson's 1940s vintage home. The total seclusion in the midst of fifteen impenetrable wooded acres returned Hitchcock to the happy years of his boyhood when his father was alive.

He prepaid the next two month's apartment rent and gave his key to Walker, who needed a place of his own.

After moving his few furnishings in, he built a crackling fire in the fireplace, brewed a pot of coffee and put his feet up as he got into a good book. At last he had digs as nonconforming as himself. All he needed now was a dog.

* * *

In the King County Jail in Seattle, Colin Wilcox sat in his cell, thinking and looking at the walls. He knew what he was, a criminal, but he took pride in being a *professional* criminal. He chose crime as a career, knowing that arrest and confinement would be occupational hazards. Wilcox had no regrets. He thought of himself as a soldier of fortune. He never blamed his behavior on his childhood, teachers or parents and regarded those who did as weak snivelers. It was a paradox that Wilcox was from a stable home, grew up on a family farm in the Yakima Valley with church-going parents and three siblings, of whose deep grief he was the chief cause.

Unlike most people, Wilcox was incapable of feelings for others and remorse for his actions. He fit psychologists' definition of a sociopath.

Wilcox always worked diligently to be the best in whatever crime specialty he chose. As he progressed from daytime home burglary to commercial burglary, he researched the richest and easiest targets, studied police methods of evidence gathering and crime prevention, security patrols and alarms. For a time he even held a job as an apprentice locksmith just to learn safecracking. He applied the same ethos when he added robbery and murder-for-hire to his repertoire because the money was better. Wilcox was a short on talk, long on action type. When he wasn't in jail or prison he practiced police style combat shooting and kept his guns clean and tuned. In the Walla Walla penitentiary he learned knife fighting and bare-hand killing techniques. He played his cards close to the vest, never confiding in anyone and never bragging about himself.

Wilcox never mocked or taunted policemen. Only punks did that. His grudging respect for the police was born of career experience. He considered most of them worthy adversaries. But times were changing. Wilcox' breed of criminal was fading away. Even in the underworld, the new anarchy was sweeping aside the old order, replacing it with a new breed of criminal: politicized, drug-addicted, pseudo-revolutionary, hateful of "The Establishment."

The way the bust went down stymied Wilcox: the officers' arrival at Charlie's was *too* timely—he considered they might have been tipped off. He knew their shift hours and patrol patterns from weeks of surveillance. Only his client knew his plan. But no, there was too much the police *didn't* know for him to believe he had been betrayed. He chalked it up to bad luck; nothing more. His only good luck was that he was still alive because he correctly read the arresting officer. He knew this officer had killed before, wouldn't hesitate to kill again and wouldn't lose a wink over it; he saw it in his eyes.

State holds for parole violation and felony possession of a firearm were pending, but Wilcox wasn't worried; to the contrary, he relaxed because of the phone call he made after booking - it wasn't to his uncle in Yakima.

* * *

As spring follows winter, seasons of peace and renewal follow seasons of war and loss. Almost en masse, the latest crop of young officers, (most of whom were vets) when probation was past, married and settled down. More often than not their brides were girls they met on the job: police records clerks, court clerks, dispatchers, bank tellers and waitresses, eager to tie the knot and make babies.

The progression repeated over and over: weddings, starter homes bought on the G.I. Bill, housewarming parties, baby showers; new arrivals thereafter. Older unwed, matronly clerks shook their heads dubiously and tsk-tsked, "My, what fertile-turtles we have here."

None of it was for Hitchcock. The "Dear John" letter from his fiancée, Ruby Cain, while he was ducking bullets and saving wounded comrades in the jungle, soured him on marriage; maybe permanently. He tried getting her back once when he was on home on leave, but it was over: Ruby was dating others—many others. Over time, he got over his hurt and bitterness. Hitchcock loved his freedom. He missed the solid family life he grew up in, but he could come and go as he pleased, and pursuing police work is his only passion.

Hitchcock wasn't lonely. His virile good looks and easy manliness naturally attracted women young and old. Currently he dated two women, each the type any man would fall on his sword to have: well-dressed, educated, classy career types. Eve, a prosecutor with the city attorney's office, a tall, trim, creamy-skinned brunette, elegantly dressed, with an outgoing personality. And Rhonda, an emergency room physician at Overlake Hospital, an attractive no-nonsense, womanly, freckle-faced, ash-blond cowgirl type who did not hide her attraction to Hitchcock.

Every Friday, Hitchcock honored his mom, Myrna, by dressing up and taking her for lunch at the Rhododendron Room in the Frederick & Nelson store in Bellevue Square.

And Myrna never failed to chide her only son during those times.

"Roger, you know your dad would have wanted you to be in medical school by now. Like him, you'd be so well suited for medicine. In high school you always got A's in biology and chemistry and your father was so proud, he felt sure you would follow in his footsteps one day. He wouldn't have wanted you in the Army, let alone on the police force, of all things," she said, shaking her head.

"But Mom, I *am* following Dad's lead — remember he left medical school during the war to join the Army. And where was he? On the beach at Normandy on D-Day, as a medic. He was even wounded there, remember?"

"Oh yes, but that was a different time. We were dating then and I was so upset with Ted for leaving medical school to go fight in a war. He could have gotten killed!" Myrna said with a dismissive wave of her hand.

"And, you should be thinking about starting a family — while you're still so young. If you're past your fling with that ... that *woman* who dumped you while you were a soldier, I've got just the girl for you, a nice girl from a good family. They go to our church. And as you know, your sisters and I don't think this police business is for you. Besides the poor pay, it's dangerous. I hear policemen aren't popular anymore, which of course is really too bad. What is this world coming to, anyway? So, Roger, the best thing is for you to get out of that uniform, get back into college, and let me introduce you to the Chatterton girl. Oh, I almost forgot—when you meet her, don't mention anything about being a boxer, just baseball. Her family's totally opposed to violence, even in sports. And don't talk about your arresting people, either."

Inwardly Hitchcock shook his head. *Mom, Mom, oh Mom,* he commented mentally. Rather than argue, he changed the subject in order to respectfully resist her never-ending motherly efforts to reattach her apron strings. After lunch he took Myrna home and did chores around her place before leaving. He checked on Allie by phone before going to the gym, (he had considered returning to the ring, but that would mean trips to Seattle for training, and giving up smoking) and spent the evening with Eve. On Saturdays he typically slept as late as possible and read Hemingway, Steinbeck, O.Henry or Poe and worked out in preparation for the busiest night of the week.

Saturday nights are often wild and fast-paced for the Patrol Division, stretching the manpower of a nine-man squad beyond capacity to answer non-emergency calls. The ringing of cash registers in the bars and no-tell motels went on without letup until after 2 a.m. Taxis ferried alcohol and call girls to private parties, officers refereed and broke up parking lot fights, traffic units and ambulances were called to accidents, and underage drinking parties spiraled out of control. Pot, cocaine and heroin were consumed conspicuously in public, while in the bars live rock and country music bands pounded and pulsed, and drunk drivers abounded on city streets. It was like musical cuffs all night—handcuffs were applied, removed at the station, and reapplied to someone else.

When station holding cells were overflowing with prisoners, two officers had to be taken off the streets for transport to the county jail in Seattle, seriously reducing officer safety. This was to the pleasure of the Third Shift, for it proved the city's need for them and refuted the city manager's scornful comments.

By 2 a.m., when the streets were clearing and Walker was transporting a prisoner to Seattle, Hitchcock got a different kind of call:

"Radio to Three Zero Six, respond to a report of a completed suicide at 25959 SE 37th Street. The Medical Examiner's Office has been called, Sgt. Breen will assist."

Hitchcock arrived at the split-level home in less than five minutes. The front door was ajar. The familiar sounds of unspeakable grieving within beckoned him to the door.

"Hello inside the house! Police officer! I'm coming in!"

He entered, the stairs creaking with each step. A grief stricken woman in her fifties lay in a fetal position on the kitchen floor, groaning and sobbing uncontrollably, tears streaming over her pain-contorted face. Her husband knelt gently over her, doing his best to console her.

Deeply moved, Hitchcock knelt next to the man, and, putting his hand on his shoulder, quietly told him, "I am here for you, sir. How can I help?"

Looking briefly at Hitchcock, the man tightly gripped his shoulder, the depth of his pain so severe Hitchcock felt it pierce him. "It's our son," he said haltingly, gasping through tears, "we came home tonight and found him dead. He's downstairs … in his room …," the broken father's voice trailed off.

He went down two short staircases to the basement. What he saw caused him to choke up. A young man in his twenties hung by his neck from a rope tied to the ceiling, his feet dangling about twenty inches above the floor. He wore a military haircut and Marine Corps dress greens. The scene told of a well planned self-execution, carried out in detail: he used the pointed compass saw, now laying on the floor, to cut holes in the ceiling on either side of the ceiling joist, around which he looped one end of a length of half-inch manila rope. He fashioned a loop with a slip-knot in the other end, stood on a chair, put the rope around his neck and kicked the chair away. Purplish post-mortem lividity was evident about his neck, face and hands. Unseeing eyes were half-open slits, and his tongue protruded from his contorted face, purplish black.

Hitchcock touched his hands, they were cold. The room temperature was sixty-eight. Placing his hand under the Marine's armpit, he judged from the fading body heat death occurred between two and four hours ago.

A handwritten note was pinned to the lapel of his uniform jacket. Hitchcock could read it without removing it:

"Mom and Dad, Please forgive me for this and try to understand. I have chosen to go be with my unit, where I belong. I love you both, Kyle."

Hitchcock, deeply affected and suppressing a surge of emotion, returned to the parents upstairs, where the father told him: "Our son joined the Marines against our wishes. He is our only child. He wanted to be a Marine since he was a boy. When his unit was transferred to Vietnam two years ago, my wife was beside herself. She has an uncle who is a congressman who pulled some strings to get our boy back home, against his wishes. The day after he left Vietnam, his entire unit was wiped out in an ambush. Kyle never forgave us, and he never got over his guilt. Back here at home, he was called a baby-killer, even by his school friends. Counseling never helped. Now we are ...," his voice trailed off.

The impact of this had Hitchcock's blood running hot. It all returned, searing memories of death and dying in the jungles of Vietnam, his anger at society, especially at the press, who sneeringly ignored and dishonored better men than themselves and made heroes of cowardly draft dodgers and glorified potheads and flag desecrators. Sergeant Breen and the medical examiner's investigator arrived, and, upon learning of the situation, Breen directed radio to have the police chaplain respond to the scene.

Someone had to honor this young man, even if posthumously. Hitchcock got his eight-point billed hat from his car and returned to the body, where stood at attention, holding a salute as the medical investigator and Sergeant Breen took the body down. After helping the medical examiner cover and remove the body from the house, Hitchcock remained with the parents until the police chaplain arrived.

Hitchcock's rawest emotions returned in force. He felt depleted; he wanted to go home to face them alone. Like the dead Marine, he had left Vietnam, but Vietnam would never leave him. He needed to get away. It was a struggle to advise radio he was back in service. Luckily, the remaining calls were few and minor. The squad would be meeting at Jason Allard's for post-shift drinking, a frequent event usually lasting up to five hours. Even Walker, whose divorce was days away from becoming final, would be going. But Hitchcock declined. He wanted solitude.

At home, removing his gun belt and uniform, Hitchcock locked the door and drew the blinds, unplugged the phone, got a glass tumbler and a bottle of Old No. 7. He turned out the lights and sat in his underwear and socks on the couch, drinking in the dark, grieving for the dead young Marine, a patriot cheated out of fulfilling his code of honor, and for his parents, who did the cheating, but out of love for their only son. There were no winners; only losers. The parents were as good as dead, they would never recover from the loss; the enormity was too much. As he refilled his glass, his musings took him back, as he knew they would, to the faces of Phu Loi, the comrades he had been unable to save, the screams of wounded and dying soldiers, men he knew by name, the pitiful villagers they treated — against orders, out of compassion, and the enemies he himself slew, until his head spun and sleep overtook him where he sat.

5

WOMANLY INTUITION

A knock-knock-knocking at the sliding glass door brought Hitchcock back from the jungle. The daylight hurt his eyes, his throat felt dry, his t-shirt sagged with sweat from dreams he couldn't recall. It was almost 1 p.m. and he was still on the couch. The knocking continued. A light rapping it was; a woman, no doubt. He peered out the window to see Rhonda there. She was dressed in a figure-hugging black sweater dress, high-heels, and pearl necklace. Usually she was in hospital scrubs or jeans and western-style flannel shirts when he saw her.

"Hi, Babe," she smiled when he opened the door. "I just got out of church and came by to take you to breakfast."

"Sure, but I have to shower first," he said, squinting.

Not one to stand on ceremony, Rhonda stepped inside and looked around. "Hmmm. Had a little one-man party after work, did we?" she said, eyeing the near-empty bottle, whiskey glass and full ashtray. "Hit the shower while I tidy up and get some coffee going," she said as she briefly caressed his shoulder. She stepped back. "Yup, you need a shower, my love," she said with a gentle push.

He showered and dressed quickly, skipping the shave to save time. Rhonda's surprise visit pleased him; she had country-girl charm, a sort of frontier openness that warmed and brightened everyone she met. She was attractive and sensual, beautiful in a rustic sort of way; tall and large-boned yet womanly and voluptuous; a well educated professional but having a down-home humility; warm and friendly but selective in her associations. Rhonda was open-hearted, in tune with herself, and decisive. Above all, her heart was set on Hitchcock.

He escorted her to her new Suburban and climbed into the passenger seat. "Where're we off to?" he asked.

"You'll see," she smiled.

He respectfully looked her over as she drove. She was a good-looking woman, well put together, and being with her rejuvenated him.

"I like it when you dress like this," he commented appreciatively.

She smiled again, taking her eyes off the road to glance at him. "Thanks. It's for church, and you. Not necessarily in that order."

As if he couldn't feel any better, her last comment flooded him with well-being as she turned into a parking lot, stopping in front of a small, one-story brick house converted into a restaurant. He had been so absorbed with Rhonda he didn't know where he was.

As if she could read his mind, Rhonda announced, "We're in Redmond, Roger. My friends own this place and they're expecting us."

True to the knightly manners he was raised with, he opened the driver door and the restaurant door for her. A plump, pleasant-looking Italian woman in her forties greeted Rhonda with a smile and a hug. The place had closed an hour ago but opened for Rhonda, who introduced Roger as they were seated.

The meal was a smorgasbord of small samplings of Italian dishes, all of it sumptuous. It was a treat for Hitchcock; far outclassing the crude man-chow he lived on. He glanced at Rhonda as she ate; she was thirty, seven years older than he, but looked younger. He recalled how they both laughed when a waiter asked for her ID when she ordered a glass of wine on their first date. Like him, she had never been married, but her reasons were different: medical school and internship.

Hitchcock was quiet, but Rhonda wanted to talk. "You never talk about Vietnam. You were a medic there. You must have seen a lot," she said, "is it okay for me to ask about it?"

Hitchcock looked down, toying with his fork, and shrugged. "Not much to tell. I was there twice, stationed in what was sort of a mini-MASH unit out of Long Binh. It was in the jungle — sort of an E.R. closer to the battlefields — to treat the wounded before getting them to the hospital at Long Binh. We operated under crude conditions. There were South Vietnamese medical personnel there too, for their soldiers. I don't know what has happened to it now."

Respecting his reluctance, Rhonda changed the subject. "My parents ranch in Davenport, near Spokane. I grew up doing ranch work with my three brothers, working on horseback, roping and moving cattle. Two of my brothers were Marines — one, Ed, was killed in Vietnam in '68. It's a loss none of us will get over. I'm the only one of four kids to get a college scholarship, which took me all the way through medical school. I like the culture here but miss the simplicity of ranch life and the drier climate. For now, at least, medicine is my calling. How I ever got into being an E.R. specialist I don't know, but I love it."

"My turn to ask a question," Hitchcock ventured.

"Fire away."

"The first time we saw each other was when I brought a rape victim into the E.R. You gave me your name and home phone number on a piece of paper within minutes. How come?"

Rhonda shrugged. "I had been turning down date offers for a long time — three years or so. I was into medical school and my career. Not one of them seemed right. The second I saw you, I wanted you. Simple as that. My turn now — why did you call me the next day?"

"Same reason — I was attracted, *and* flattered."

As the meal was ending, Rhonda looked at her watch, a plain silver case with white dial and brown leather strap — the kind people expect doctors and nurses to wear.

"I know you have to work tonight, so let's skip dessert. I have a surprise for you," she said.

When the bill came Hitchcock took it from her. "It's my treat, Roger," she protested.

"You're a girl, aren't'cha?"

Breaking into a broad grin, quick-witted Dr. Rhonda quipped, "Aye. As only thou knowest so well, m'lord!"

Hitchcock couldn't help smiling ear-to-ear as he fished cash out of his wallet and gave it to the waiter.

Rhonda's place was in the woods east of Redmond, a rustic one-story log house with a small barn and pasture in the back. Once in the front door she put her arms around him and kissed him briefly.

"Wait here with your eyes closed," she commanded lovingly, "no peeking."

He heard her go out the back door and return in a moment.

"Okay, you can look now."

Before him was a handsome adult German Shepherd mix. His back, sides and head were black, with silver belly, chest and throat. Oddly, his eyes were blue-green instead of brown and his tail curled up over his back, indicating possible Husky blood in the mix. He was lean, deep-chested and large-boned. Hitchcock guessed his weight at maybe seventy pounds. He extended his hand, palm down, for the dog to sniff; the dog sniffed the hand, reservedly at first, and looked up at Hitchcock, wagging his tail slightly in acceptance.

"His name is Jamie. My cousin Karl owned a fenced construction equipment lot out in the east county that had a lot of break-ins until he got Jamie—after Jamie chewed up a couple guys who climbed over the fence at night there weren't any more thefts."

"Why is he getting rid of him?"

"Karl closed the place last month to retire. Jamie needs a new home now. I've been holding him here for you about a month. He's housebroken and I got all his shots updated. He's too good to wind up at the pound. He also gets along with my dogs, by the way. We should be heading back to Bellevue now," she said handing him the leash. Hitchcock, grinning with pleasure, took the leash, bent down and ran his hands roughly over Jamie's shoulders and neck, working up to his head, all of which the dog leaned into as a token of respect for his new master. For man and dog, visceral needs were mutually fulfilled

"How did you know, and how can I thank you, Rhonda?" Hitchcock asked when they returned to his cabana.

As she slipped her arm around his neck, they held each other and kissed again, fully this time. "I'm a woman, that's how I knew. I have to go now, but as for thanking me I'm sure you will come up with something that will be acceptable to me, Mr. Hitchcock."

Hitchcock felt his heart warming as Rhonda left. He wondered if the numbness would ever thaw enough for him to love again. If it ever happened, it would take time.

6

NEW TROUBLE IN OLD TOWN

As superb a patrol officer as Clive Brooks was, it was ironic that while his felony arrests were consistently at or near the top every month and the citizens of his downtown beat liked and respected him, within the Department he was almost invisible. He worked his beat pro-actively and by the book. He was attentive to detail. Citizen complaints against Brooks were rare as hen's teeth. Though born and raised in Seattle, his appearance and demeanor reflected his British military heritage (his family came over from England on military defense work with Boeing). Fair-complexioned, of slender frame and medium height, his square-shouldered bearing; short, wavy, light brown hair; trim mustache and piercing pale blue eyes made him seem so British. Because he sometimes stuttered and talked more than he should, his fellow officers nicknamed him "Babbling Brooks."

Brooks seldom talked about himself. Few people knew he was awarded the Silver Star for bravery as an Air Policeman guarding the air field of the Tan Son Nhut air base in Vietnam during the heaviest fighting between 1968and 1969. He wasn't the dominate bone-and-muscle type most of his brother officers were. His brawn, frame and combat skills were average at best, but what he lacked in these departments he made up for with bravery; he never failed to give a good account of himself in a fight, was never one to back down.

Brooks' unique sixth sense for spotting stolen cars amazed his peers. He would park at the corner of an intersection, watching cars go by until, for no discernible reason, he dropped the gear shift into drive, flipped the overhead red dome light on, pull a car over, and sure enough, it was stolen. By this talent alone he usually led the department in felony arrests every month.

Brooks' briefcase was always crammed with copies of the latest stolen car list known as the "hot sheet" and copies of the Western States Crime Bulletin, which reported on the movements and methods of professional shoplift rings, safecrackers, burglary teams and armed robbery gangs roaming the West, the names and faces of which he memorized.

The brass wisely assigned Brooks to District One, the commercial downtown core, where he was the traditional neighborhood beat cop who knew everybody, like a caring uncle. He worked hand-in-glove with the store detectives of the Nordstrom Best and Frederick & Nelson stores of Bellevue Square. Thus, over time it came to be that District One was Clive Brooks, and Clive Brooks was District One. But neither he nor anyone else on the Department could have foreseen the nature of the moment of fame that was headed Brooks' way.

Between Bellevue's downtown and its upscale neighborhoods there existed a thin ring of run-down, '50s vintage apartments, abandoned houses, sheds and shanty motels that became the haunts of a new generation of criminals — home-grown drug addicts, school dropouts from upscale families in their late teens and early twenties — who lived by preying on their neighbors. For reasons not clear, the sharp increase of residential and commercial burglaries, and car prowls west if the 405 freeway escaped the notice of the newly created Crime Analysis Unit.

Two trends were on a collision course: Bellevue was acquiring a reputation among criminals as the place to avoid because of its aggressive police, while in academia the hot topic of debate was whether cops should continue to be legally allowed to shoot fleeing felons if the felony presents no safety threat. It would be through Brooks that the ice would be broken.

Past 11 p.m. on the last Sunday in September, a quiet Indian Summer evening of crisp air and clear skies, the sort of weather that carries sound almost as well as fog. Brooks, sitting in his patrol car in an alley off Main Street with windows down, lights and motor off, heard the sound of glass breaking, followed by three or four clanging sounds of metal-on-metal.

Turning the radio volume down, he keyed the mike and reported softly. "Three Zero One, radio. I hear glass breaking in the vicinity of 103rd and Main, in Old Town. Requesting backup to investigate."

"Three Zero Three will respond to Three Zero One's location, Radio," LaPerle transmitted.

Dispatch acknowledged LaPerle. Brooks keyed the radio mike and whispered. "Three Zero One to Three Zero Three, the sounds came from one of the businesses along the south side of Main Street in Old Town, east of 102nd Avenue. I'll be on foot. Drive slowly westbound on Main. I will see you."

Brooks gathered his baton and flashlight, locked his cruiser and crossed Main Street. There was no traffic as he hunted in silence along the rear service entrances of Main Street shops and diners. He stopped frequently, passing town icons Toys Café, the Bellevue Barber Shop, and the Black Magic tavern, briefly inspecting the few parked cars there were. None were warm to the touch.

Westward among shadows, on full alert, listening intently for more sounds to lead him to their source, Brooks crept slowly along the backs of two other closed-up shops. When he reached the back of Lakeside Drugs, he knew this was the scene. Heart pounding, Brooks reached the corner of the drugstore and peeked around. The lights were out. The glass window to the left of the service door had been smashed out; the door was wide open. He could hear LaPerle's patrol car idling along Main Street on the opposite side of the drugstore as he approached the rear door, revolver at the ready. When LaPerle's spotlight flooded the drugstore front to back, a crashing sound erupted inside, followed by a lone male figure running through the rear service door.

"Stop - Police!" Brooks shouted. The suspect ran wide enough around him to stay out of arms' reach. Gripping his Smith and Wesson .38 in both hands, Brooks took aim as the suspect sprinted across the lighted rear parking lot, heading for the shadows beyond. "You are under arrest! Stop or I'll shoot!" Brooks shouted as he aimed and squeezed off a shot—the blast shattered the night calm.

Seeing no indication his bullet found its mark, Brooks took aim and fired a second shot. The suspect staggered briefly and almost fell. He resumed his flight, disappearing into the shadows.

When LaPerle, nicknamed "Frenchie" by his peers, on the other side of the drugstore from Brooks, heard the shots, he immediately radioed "shots fired." Within a half hour the trickle of other officers and the on-duty supervisor to the scene began, soon to become a flood of detectives, departmental brass and reporters. Detectives found no identified latent prints in the store, which had no alarm.

A short trail of blood led south for a few feet. A search of the area yielded nothing. None of the area hospitals reported receiving anyone with a gunshot wound, thus the crime would go unsolved - for the time being.

But Brooks, though he got only a glimpse of the suspect in the dark in the excitement of the moment, told detectives who he thought it was.

Nearly every Bellevue officer had contacted or arrested Mitchell Mark Jolnes at one time or another. Now at the age of twenty, he was a prominent figure in the under-realm of young, homegrown, drug dependent petty thieves plaguing West Bellevue, of which he was a native son. Cops from Bellevue and surrounding communities had been arresting Jolnes for a widening range of crimes since he was a juvenile. He lived on the run, homeless, drifting from homes of friends and girlfriends to sheds to abandoned houses to camps in the woods, stealing and leeching off parents and friends, rarely leaving West Bellevue. But now a police manhunt for him was on.

Jolnes disappeared.

The story was front page news in the weekly *Bellevue American,* the city's only newspaper. A firestorm of criticism erupted when the paper disclosed the suspect escaped with a large quantity of prescription drugs and hundreds in cash from the safe. The paper followed up with a series of investigative articles detailing the recent rise in downtown crime, mounting citizen complaints to the police administration and the alleged failure to address the problem.

An avalanche of angry letters to the editor from downtown business owners appeared in the paper, citing instances of tepid police response to their complaints. When the downtown business community appeared en masse at the next city council meeting, laying out their frustrations and complaints, the city manager, well known for public cop-hating remarks such as "the police are but a necessary nuisance in a decent community," stated he would hold the Department and Chief Carter accountable.

The Department's response was swift in coming. Authorization for an increased budget for two-man foot patrol teams, portable radios and overtime pay for officers willing to work overtime were launched to supplement the car units in the downtown. Officers from detectives, traffic, crime analysis and station units quickly signed up with patrol officers wanting a full shift of overtime. The roster for the next three months was filled in a day, and Hitchcock, eager to try foot patrol, and wanting overtime pay for the coming holidays, put himself on the list.

7

BLUE VENGEANCE

It was Friday when an angry hush swept over each shift briefing how Officer Ronny Austin, of the rural Carnation Police Department, took his life days after the prosecution declined to file charges against Jim McMinn and Crawford Beecham for what they did to him.

Home to the whistle-stop burgs of Fall City, Carnation, Snoqualmie, North Bend and Duvall, the Snoqualmie Valley was a rural region of East King County given to small family-run dairy farms in the lowlands, small lumber mills and logging in the foothills. The deep woods of the foothills havened Ozark-style moonshine operations run by homegrown, deadly hillbillies like McMinn and Beecham These stout, tough, young woodsmen lived on the edge of law and society as poachers of deer and elk, timber pirates who harvested fir and cedar from private woodlands they sold to small mill operations, and they sold their illegal 200-proof booze, locally known as "everclear" or "white lightning," to local bars that poured it into labeled liquor bottles to cut their costs, unbeknownst to the customers.

McMinn and Beecham, both of mixed Indian descent, lived as men from an earlier century. Like old-time outlaws, they shared the same cabin and the same women from the local reservation and lived by looting and intimidation. Each was an experienced barroom brawler and hunter, each kept a rifle and a chainsaw in the cab of his pickup, carried a revolver on his belt, and openly scorned the new generation of cops as soft sissies. They especially loathed Ronny Austin, a man too short and slight to meet the height-weight standards of larger metropolitan police agencies.

Hitchcock, who was there off-duty for downtown foot patrol, was angered by the circumstances of Austin's death. He remembered meeting Austin once when he picked up a prisoner from him. Austin was the desk officer at the time, and Hitchcock enjoyed several minutes of friendly shop-talk with him. Hitchcock didn't know Austin was a fellow Army vet, an infantryman who was decorated for bravery during the 1968 Tet offensive.

The devil was in the details of how Austin died, and gruesome details they were. It happened months earlier, close to 3 AM on a Monday. McMinn and Beecham were parked in front of a closed tavern, facing the street, sitting in Beecham's pickup, drinking whiskey from the bottle with a girl from the reservation sitting between them. Officer Austin was on routine patrol when he stopped to inquire of their business. Exactly what happened next was a matter of conjecture, for neither the two men nor the girl would talk, and Austin was too traumatized to give a coherent account, but the town awoke the next morning to find Officer Austin completely naked, beaten and bleeding, cuffed with his own handcuffs to a telephone pole on the corner of the main intersection, his badge removed from his uniform shirt and pinned through the flesh of his exposed buttocks. For hours, citizens drove by on their way to work, staring but not offering assistance. School buses went by, kids yelling and jeering, forever breaking the spirit of the man who had taken an oath to serve and protect them after so valiantly risking his life to serve his country. For Hitchcock and the others, it was a sobering reality-check of where they really stood with the people they were sworn to protect

Friday was Clive Brooks' night off, making Mark Forbes the District One car. Hitchcock, having cancelled a dinner date with Eve for a chance for overtime pay in advance of the holidays, was pleased to be paired for foot patrol with Lee Wooten, an academy classmate. Wooten was a tough Montana cowboy, a Navy swiftboat veteran of two one-year tours in Vietnam. After briefing they checked out portable radios and were dropped off in the center of their beat, the north half of downtown. It was 9 p.m.

In the bar of the Village Inn restaurant on the northwest corner of NE 8th Street and 104th Avenue, (the main downtown intersection), McMinn and Beecham sat on bar stools drinking with another man; a small, refined weasel in a suit. The three celebrated a court victory. McMinn shoved an envelope stuffed with bills across the bar top to the shyster.

"Here's your fee, paid in full. Thanks for getting us out of this," he said, as Beecham nodded in agreement.

Smiling like a Cheshire cat, the scumbag lawyer quickly counted the bills in the envelope before slipping it into his inside jacket pocket. "Always glad to help anyone who hates cops the way I do," he said. Knocking down the last of his drink, as he turned to leave, he advised: "Be careful in this town — cops here are pretty aggressive."

But McMinn and Beecham were feeling too cocky, too on top of the world to take such advice. "We can handle 'em," was their response. They had come to Bellevue to see their attorney after his meeting in Seattle with the prosecutor's office. All charges were withdrawn due to "insufficient evidence." The two thugs' campaign of witness intimidation had paid off - because of their reputations for retaliation, the general community was too afraid to testify against them. They continued drinking and gloating over their victory, clinking their glasses together in a toast to Austin's death.

As their glasses were being refilled for the third time, two young couples entered, heading for a table. One of the women was especially attractive, and McMinn, feeling his firewater, turned on his barstool and whistled long and loud, followed by loud Indian war yelps as she passed by. Her escort — a pasty-faced, slender hippy-type wearing bellbottom jeans, a Paisley-print shirt with over-size collar, long dark Beatle-type hairstyle, meekly protested, "Hey man, let's cool it."

"'Hey man, cool it?' Is that what you said, punk?" jeered McMinn. "Come over here and say that and see how long you're on your feet! Then I'll take her for myself! Maybe we'll both have her. What'll you say about that, boy?"

Frozen with fear, knowing he was totally outmatched by these human animals, he stood speechless, trembling under his shirt. The bartender broke in. "Okay, you two. That's enough. Get out of here now or I'll call the cops."

"Go ahead, call 'em!" Beecham snorted. "We beat the last cop who crossed us so bad he's dead now, so send 'em to us!"

Sergeant Lane Baxter happened to be in the restaurant, off duty, with his wife He tried to intervene. Perhaps it was out of a sense of kinship when they saw Lane's obvious Indian heritage that they hesitated. If so, it was momentary.

McMinn and Beecham nodded to each other as they accepted Baxter's invitation to step outside to talk. In the open area of the front parking lot the three men stood. Baxter calmly offered to call them a cab; they refused and said they were going back inside.

"No wait," Baxter said. "Let me show you something."

Showing his police badge, Baxter started to speak when Beecham slipped behind him as McMinn glared menacingly and said, "I'm McMinn and my partner's Beecham. We beat little Officer Ronny so bad he killed himself, and you're next!"

Beecham pulled Baxter's windbreaker back and down so it bound his arms, making him defenseless as McMinn punched him hard in the solar plexus, forcing the wind out of his lungs with a wheezing sound as he doubled over. They began punching Baxter on his head and body. As he began to crumple, his wife Gloria, came screaming through the front door, arms flailing. "Stop! Oh God, Stop!"

McMinn punched her in the mouth, knocking her to the pavement, bleeding and unable to get up.

A crowd from the restaurant gathered outside and cowered in fear as they watched a helpless Baxter being beaten and kicked by two savage men; no one daring to help. Beecham glared at the crowd. "Which of you lily-white cowards wants to be next?"

Approaching sirens were heard. The first unit to arrive was Mark Forbes, a short but fit officer who had never been in a fight. Forbes bailed out of his car to engage Beecham in an effort to save Sergeant Baxter. With one punch Beecham cratered Forbes' nose, causing him to buckle as blood gushed. McMinn kicked his legs out from under him and began kicking him in the ribs when he fell. Hitchcock and Wooten arrived on foot as the second unit. McMinn seized Forbes' baton and struck Wooten twice as he drew his baton, snapping his collarbone. Joel Otis, perhaps the most admired and feared officer on the Bellevue PD, arrived in a cruiser and faced McMinn, who began swinging the baton wildly, hatefully taunting and challenging Otis.

Taller, beefier, heavier-boned and perhaps stronger than Hitchcock, Beecham prepared for Hitchcock's advance. Surging with adrenalin, alcohol and blood lust, uttering Indian war whoops as he started a wild windmill with his fists, he faced Hitchcock.

Choosing his fists over his baton, (exactly what the brass told officers *not* to do), Hitchcock flipped his hat aside as he waded in, intentional destruction and punishment in every step, heading straight at Beecham.

Hitchcock's experience of over a hundred fights in Golden Gloves boxing and disciplined fitness regimen now came into play. Moving straight in, bending slightly at the waist, hands guarding his head, he skillfully slipped between Beecham's wild punches untouched, closing in and landing a left jab as he was pushing off with his right foot, adding his shoulder and entire body weight to the jab. It landed squarely on Beecham's nose, crushing it, rocking him back, blood flowed immediately and Beecham knew he was going down. The surprise on his face at the bone-breaking power of the punch changed to fear when, before he could react, Hitchcock closed in tighter, almost forehead-to-forehead, and fired a right uppercut into his sternum and solar plexus that lifted him off his heels, followed by a left hook to the jaw that felled him like a tree. Hitchcock stood over Beecham as he rolled to one side in an effort to get up and fight back. Bending slightly from the waist, he rained his right fist like a missile onto Beecham's jawbone; a snap was heard as Beecham collapsed again, jaw hanging open, mouth and nose bleeding, conscious, trying but unable to rise, utterly crushed in seconds.

McMinn, meanwhile, was no match for Otis. Having been cut down in seconds by Otis' baton, he too was on the pavement, retching and holding his stomach, his head covered in his own blood, while more blood bubbled from his open mouth with every breath. Otis, of course, was unscathed.

The medic in Hitchcock checked on Gloria Baxter first, who was returning to consciousness, and then to Lane Baxter, who advised through his blood-covered face "these are the two who beat Austin in Carnation this year. They were in the bar bragging about it before they attacked me."

This news made Hitchcock want to punish McMinn and Beecham further, but no - they were done; the battle was over. It was mop-up time. A two-man ambulance crew stood outside their hearse at Bob Osberg's Texaco across NE 8th from the scene, waiting until it was safe to attend to the injured, while the siren of a second approaching ambulance could be heard.

Surveying the scene—five bleeding bodies lying on the pavement—Hitchcock waved the ambulance crew in. He forbade them to attend to Beecham and McMinn, directing them to tend to Gloria Baxter and the injured officers first, allowing McMinn and Beecham to lay, disabled, bones broken, in their own blood; the power of their animality destroyed. Neither would be the same again.

8

TWISTS AND TURNS

Shocking news awaited Hitchcock the following Monday at shift briefing: somehow, Colin Wilcox walked. It happened over the weekend. An attorney representing Wilcox appeared before a county District Court Judge, who, whether through ignorance or deliberate disregard for the state's parole violation hold and pending firearms possession charge, released him upon the posting of ten thousand dollars cash bond. The county jail claimed it had no knowledge of additional holds. Who the attorney was and who posted such a high bond, no one seemed to know.

Hitchcock prided himself as being intellectually above "conspiracy behind every bush" thinking, but the timely release of a career criminal wanted on parole violation forced him to reconsider District Six: If freeing a reputed hit man like Wilcox justified posting five-figure money through hush-hush back room dealings, it meant organized crime is pursuing interests in his district. He realized he is not in the know ... somehow he to be.

Lane and Gloria Baxter spent a full day under observation at the hospital where docs monitored them for signs of brain injury. Lane, generally regarded by the rank-and-file as the most popular sergeant in Patrol Division, sustained multiple contusions to his face, head and ribs. Gloria sustained head and neck injuries from being punched and hitting her head on the sidewalk. Lee Wooten's right collarbone had been fractured in the baton fight with McMinn. Mark Forbes had a broken nose and bruised ribs, back, and legs.

McMinn and Beecham were still being held at Harborview County Hospital with injuries to their heads, internal organs and broken bones. The prosecutor's office wasted no time filing multiple charges of felony assault. Public outrage being what it was, they were beyond the help of their dirtbag attorney. For them, it would be years of prison time.

In another welcome twist of justice, the rifle and revolver found in McMinn's pickup when it was impounded were both reported stolen, and the prints of both McMinn and Beecham were on each weapon. Hitchcock went even further in his quest for justice for Ron Austin: he phoned both Steve Miller, a cub reporter with the Bellevue paper, and the feds to tip off where McMinn and Beecham had their whiskey still, triggering news stories and more charges, state and now federal.

Thanks to the solid journalism of the Bellevue and Kirkland papers, the fallout from the fight in front of the Village Inn was positive. Hitchcock and Otis declined interviews with reporters, yet the weekly *Bellevue American* carried the full story, focusing on McMinn and Beecham's intimidation of the state's witnesses in the Ronny Austin incident as the catalyst. Old articles of Hitchcock's Golden Gloves career were reprinted. The combined stories of Brooks shooting at a fleeing burglar and the hospitalizing of a pair of violent criminals who resisted arrest created a new tone of respect downtown, especially in the bars.

Because of the arrests by the downtown foot patrols, within a month burglary and car prowls declined drastically. This and other successes of the Patrol Division restored Chief Carter from the hot seat, temporarily frustrating the political ambitions of his detractors.

But not everyone was satisfied.

Hitchcock held a different view. He had been raised to regard policemen as their communities' representatives; an attack on an officer is an attack on the community. Therefore anyone trying to kill an officer, let alone anyone who kills an officer, deserves death. To him, the opportunity for justice to be done by permanently removing an intolerable threat to the community was missed.

Under state law and department policy, McMinn could have been justifiably shot for wielding a baton in an effort to kill or inflict severe bodily harm upon the officers with a seized baton. McMinn, Hitchcock believed, more than Beecham, deserved to pay with his life not only for what he did to Austin, but for trying to kill Otis. Killing McMinn on the spot would be sending the strongest possible message to the criminal community about trifling with Bellevue officers. He battled Beecham barehanded because Beecham was not armed, but McMinn seized one officer's baton, with which he struck down Wooten and tried to inflict serious bodily harm or kill Otis.

Yet Otis, whom Hitchcock admired and had known since childhood, did not use his gun when he had every right to.

Why? Hitchcock believed the answer was officers' distrust of the top brass and the city manager bred a "never shoot" mindset. Too often upper level of the administration tended to side with citizens who filed complaints against officers before they heard both sides of the story. Some officers believed certain superiors were especially intimidated if the citizens were college educated.

Among themselves officers speculated negatively what the brass would have done to Clive Brooks for shooting at a fleeing burglar were it not for the business community expressing their support.

Chief Sean Carter was liked by everyone. The troops liked him but regarded him as too passive for the times. The only one in the administration the troops trusted and respected was Captain Erik Delstra, a bold take-no-prisoners type whom some officers likened to General George Patton. "We'd have a *real* department, like Seattle, if Delstra was chief," the troops said among themselves. But the chances of that were slim to none. The city fathers were too afraid of controversy to take a chance on a bold leader.

It was quiet in District Six the following week, and Hitchcock, being of a new mindset in the wake of Wilcox being at large, used the calm to scrutinize his beat for abnormalities. He found them right away.

On Monday night, near midnight, he spotted a man sitting alone in a car with lights off in the Albertson's parking lot on the south side of the freeway. The car was parked facing the freeway. Something was up. Hitchcock used his binoculars. The man was using binoculars to watch the Bellevue Airport across the freeway.

The airport was closed and the runway lights were off, yet a plane approached out of the blackness and landed. Hitchcock focused his binoculars on the airport. A car came out of the shadows and met the plane on the runway. A man got out of the car, received a bulky item from the plane and returned with it to the car. In seconds the car left and the plane took to the air.

Hitchcock recognized he had just witnessed the transfer phase of a smuggling operation; the man in the parking lot was somehow involved. Hitchcock ran the plate number of the car. The registered owner had a Seattle address; there were no warrants.

Pretending he hadn't seen the drop-off at the runway, Hitchcock acted nonchalant. "Good evening, sir. Just checking to see if you're all right and what the situation is."

"Oh. Good evening, Officer. I'm just watching planes land at night. Interested in flying myself. Night landings are tricky, so I thought I'd learn by watching real landings," the man, a well-groomed business type in his forties, cordially replied.

The man's smooth over-politeness and purposely keeping his hands in sight without being told put Hitchcock on alert even further.

Hitchcock played the ignorant nice guy. "No problem sir. Can I see some ID, please?"

The address on his driver's license matched the registration.

The man's story was bunk, of course. Seattle had at least two private airfields, not to mention the international airport. The man checked clear for warrants. Hitchcock left and noted the information on a Field Interview Report card and his notebook.

It was quiet. Hitchcock re-patrolled the business district, aggressively checking cars left parked in public parking areas. Past 1 a.m. Hitchcock made his second trip around The Great Wall. It had been closed all night. Earlier, only a few lights were on inside and two cars, neither belonging to Juju, were parked at the rear. He had checked the doors then; they were locked. But now both cars were gone and all lights were out. Ordinarily this could be explained as the owner and manager doing inventory, but he had in mind Colin Wilcox's two back-to-back visits to The Great Wall just before his arrest, and Juju's lying about it. He wrote these details in his notebook.

Tuesday night. Again The Great Wall was not open. After the other bars closed and everyone went home Hitchcock and Walker decided to break up the evening with their usual form of slow night fun.

They met at the Eastside Disposal transfer site below the freeway. Leaving the window down and the radio on in one cruiser, they climbed over the chain link fence, dropping inside where mountains of garbage had been piled. Turning on their flashlights they switched the issued service ammunition for LaPerle's hand-loaded practice ammo, holstered, and aimed their flashlights at the piles in front of them. Within seconds, a large rat appeared, then another. Hitchcock aimed his flashlight at it as Walker drew and fired one round, narrowly missing. Hitchcock took his turn at the next opportunity, and thus they dueled, keeping score on rats killed versus missed. By the time they had each fired twelve rounds, they heard dispatch calling.

"Three Zero Six, and Three Zero Five, residents in the Woodridge area are reporting what sounds like shots fired in the vicinity of Richards Road near the freeway."

They climbed over the fence to their cars. Hitchcock keyed the mike. "Three Zero Six is en route, radio."

Walker radioed: "Three Zero Five radio, I am in the area. Don't hear anything."

"10-4. Both units Remain in the area. Still getting calls."

"Received, radio," Walker replied, chuckling as he reloaded duty ammo.

"You're too slow, Ira." Hitchcock told Walker. "Woman-trouble can get a man killed. I've seen it happen. Force yourself to set it aside. Women have their place with us, but they must be kept in place. Keep your head clear. Build muscle memory with your gun so that even if you are wounded your body will continue to fight on its own. You can do it at home without burning up a lot of ammo. Draw your empty gun from the holster, coming up on target in a two-hand stance, twenty-five times before every shift. Do it slowly at first, concentrate on the correct mechanics. Speed will come automatically. I know you're strapped, so I'll spring for an extra box of Frenchie's handloads when I get mine. You'll have it tomorrow."

"I'll take it. You're a buddy, Roger."

Hitchcock's mind turned to Allie. It had been days since he spoke to her and he still hadn't run the plate of her ex-husband's car or the phone number for this Jim Reynolds she told him about. Clearing the "shots fired" call after another ten minutes, Hitchcock went to a pay phone and called Records. Patty, a uniformed police matron, answered. He asked her to run the license plate of Allie's ex-husband's Mercedes, and to check out the name and phone number of Jim Reynolds.

Patty wanted to talk. "Hey, Roger, nice handling you and Otis did of those guys at the Village Inn the other night. The word is they're both still at Harborview, all busted up. I hear Beecham's jaw is wired shut and on a liquid diet through a straw. We read about your Golden Gloves career — seven first place trophies and qualified for the boxing team for the '64 Olympics. None of us here knew that about you. And, just so you know, the other night you guys were on that chase, ole Breen was pacing the dispatch center, face was blood-red, sweating bullets. We thought he would have a heart attack when your radio went "down" when it did …" she laughed knowingly. "I'll have the info in your inbox before you get off shift tonight," she promised.

After 4 a.m. Hitchcock left the station for Allie's apartment. He waited across the street. Allie's Toyota was there. While he waited, he read the information and let out a low whistle. The Mercedes Allie's ex drove was registered to a prominent family that owned several blocks of downtown Seattle; one office building bore the family name. The family address was in the most exclusive gated neighborhood in Seattle contrasted sharply with Allie's humble circumstances. Now he had questions for Allie.

The phone number Allie gave him for 'Jim Reynolds' was unlisted. To reverse it to get the subscriber name and address, the phone company required a warrant or a subpoena from a detective. There were too many Jim Reynolds in the greater metropolitan area to sort through. *Might as well be 'Bob Smith,'* Hitchcock concluded.

At 5 a.m. a middle-aged woman with hair in curlers arrived in an older sedan and went up the stairs into Allie's apartment. Hitchcock concluded she must be Allie's mom. In another minute, Allie emerged, wearing her white waitress dress under a green ski parka. Again he liked what he saw. Even in her plain white waitress uniform, her femininity was intense. He watched her descend the stairs and leave for work. His objective was to see if this 'Jim Reynolds' or anyone else followed her. No one did. He tailed her to the Pancake Corral and went in, the first customer of the day.

Allie seated him in her section so they could talk before it got busy.

9

ON THE EDGE

It was to no one's surprise when Colin Wilcox didn't show for his pre-trial hearing. No one attempted to get his car out of impound. A warrant-based search of the vehicle's contents yielded a list of phone numbers for the detectives to pursue. Wilcox's prints were on the 9mm pistol and both magazines. The weapon was not listed as stolen. Tracing from the factory by the feds would take time. The court issued a no-bail arrest warrant for Wilcox and everyone moved on to other matters.

The normal flow of calls and reports, along with a spike in drug overdose and seizures of marijuana and cocaine, overshadowed the Wilcox matter. With Wilcox at large and charges filed, there was nothing more to do but move on. Hitchcock resumed his attention to routine patrol, but with a new wariness because Wilcox was at large and the implications of big money organized crime in Eastgate, indicated by Wilcox's mysterious high-dollar walk out of the King County Jail. Hitchcock rightfully felt a sense of vulnerability, of "what's next?"

So Wilcox came to Seattle on a mission and Hitchcock's chance arrest of him interrupted it. The mission certainly wasn't armed robbery. Crime bosses don't spend ten grand to spring a robber out of jail; far less than that would he get if he robbed the whole crowd at Charlie's. It was something else, but what? With Wilcox on the loose, Hitchcock couldn't risk assuming a cold, business-like criminal like Wilcox, skilled in the use of disguises and weapons, wouldn't return to complete his mission.

At Warshall's Sporting Goods in Seattle the next afternoon, he bought a double-barrel derringer in .38 Special as a hideout gun. He had Egbert "Eggs" Voigt, leather craftsman in Issaquah who made the department's leather gear, make him an inside-the-waistband holster for the small, flat-sided two-shooter.

Safety for Charlie's was uppermost on Hitchcock's mind. He met privately, off duty with Wally Evans, expressing his concerns and developing methods for increased security including code words for Charlie's employees to use in case of emergency.

Hitchcock collected bits of information he knew were connected even though they didn't yet fit. He was confident that as more information came in, the full story would be known. Though still necessary, traditional routine patrol, the reactive policing, concerned with responding to calls was inadequate to meet the challenge of organized crime.

To be proactive, he needed a streetwise informant to work behind the scenes but he hadn't the faintest idea how to go about it; the Department was out of step with the times when it came to such matters.

A dry cold snap interrupted the returning rains the second week of November, causing the normal cloud cover to freeze and fall down. Evening temperatures in the mid-20s meant icy roads, keeping most folks inside. Thus it was odd for Hitchcock, on a traffic stop on the frontage road at 10 p.m. on a Wednesday, to see a Harley chopper with ape-hanger handlebars, ridden by a bearded biker wearing sunglasses, leaving the area behind The Great Wall, accelerating heavily along the frontage road, far over the speed limit, to the freeway overpass. He was out of sight heading east by the time Hitchcock finished.

He drove around The Great Wall. As he noted earlier, it was closed; unusual for a Wednesday. The front parking lot was empty, but strangely, two late model sedans were now parked in the back, along with Juju Kwan's Cadillac. Inside, lights were on in the back; the door was locked. As he returned to his cruiser, he received a call.

"Three Zero Six, assist the state patrol in a multiple car injury accident on eastbound I-90 east of the Eastgate overpass until they arrive. We have an ambulance on the way."

Hitchcock arrived in seconds. A flatbed truck carrying a long bundle of steel reinforcing rods, which projected several feet past the rear, was stopped on the gravel median. The driver was unhurt. Behind the truck, nose into the dirt of the median was a full-sized sedan; its windshield pierced by the steel rods that hit the driver. The ambulance arrived. The semi-conscious driver, his forehead bleeding, smelled of alcohol. In the car with him was a Doberman puppy, wounded and whimpering in pain on the back seat.

Lying ahead of the pickup and the car was the motorcycle and rider Hitchcock had seen moments earlier. The rider was conscious. The frame and front wheel of the motorcycle were bent

Hitchcock approached. "Hey man. Are you alright? Are you in pain?" he asked.

The biker had no apparent injuries. He had lightning bars tattooed on his neck and four-letter obscenities on the knuckles of both hands. His eyes widened and his face contorted with fear and hostility when he looked up at Hitchcock, standing over him.

"Get outta here, Bellevue pig!" he screamed.

"Easy now. Just trying to know what happened."

The state trooper arrived and Hitchcock stayed to help him.

The ambulance took the injured driver of the car to the E.R. Hitchcock helped the trooper restrain the biker, for whom outstanding warrants for drug possession with intent to sell, possession of stolen property and assault were confirmed. His delirium and smelling of alcohol necessitated taking him to Overlake Hospital for an involuntary blood draw.

The puppy died before the veterinarian arrived. According to the pickup driver, the accident was caused when the motorcycle passed him in the inside lane and clipped the front of his truck in an apparent effort to cut him off.

Hitchcock was the last to clear the scene, providing traffic control for tow truck drivers. He contacted the trooper at Overlake, where the biker was strapped into a gurney, incoherent, behaving wildly; results on the blood draw were expected momentarily. He was called away from the hospital on a disturbance call at the Wagon Wheel lounge in Eastgate. Obtaining the trooper's case number and phone number before leaving, Hitchcock sped to the scene, Code Two.

The fight was over and Walker had dispersed the crowd by the time Hitchcock arrived. The bartender had ordered the two brawlers outside before fists flew. The fight was brief. The winner was a regular customer everyone knew only as Josh, who left before Walker arrived. The other man had a bloody nose, refused to press charges and went home.

Most of the crowd went to their cars. Hitchcock remembered his search for a mole. Instinctively he went inside to look around. He noticed the barmaid, a pretty, buxom young brunette, who was noticing him, and smiling.

For the last hour of his shift Hitchcock checked parking lots and closed businesses along both sides of I-90. He went to the station early and called the state trooper at the hospital.

"Hitchcock, Bellevue PD, here, checking to see if there were any results on the blood work on the I-90 biker."

"Yes, officer—glad you called. His blood alcohol was point oh-eight percent, and his blood tested high for cocaine."

"Did he say anything about where he had been before the accident?" Hitchcock queried.

"Yes, as a matter of fact he did. He mentioned some Chinese joint but couldn't or wouldn't remember the name of it. He also had several hundred dollars in new bills in his wallet," the trooper reported.

"Did he say where he was drinking and doping?"

"Yes. The Chinese place for both, but he wouldn't give any details."

More pieces are starting to fit, Hitchcock realized. He got the biker's details from the trooper and thanked him before ending the call.

He devoted the afternoon of his first day off to writing a summary of the facts as he knew them, making a list of possible motives, which he narrowed to two possibilities. He looked forward to returning to work. Before his weekend ended he doubled the ammunition he expended in practice and bought a more powerful pair of binoculars.

Returning to work early, he found a handwritten, sealed envelope marked "Urgent" in his inbox. The writing was Eve's. Tucking it into his officer's notebook, he headed toward the briefing room. Sergeant Breen stopped him in the hallway.

"Roger, Lieutenant Bostwick wants to see you in his office after shift briefing. Didn't say what it was about."

Hitchcock was uneasy. He knew Bostwick hated him for no reason and was hated by the troops as an ambitious climber who was making his way up the ranks by schmoozing the brass and the city manager's office on and off the job, without ever making an arrest on his own. Bostwick in his office on a Saturday night, wearing his uniform, could only mean trouble. For no reason other than to flex his power, Bostwick had caused several promising new officers to fail their probationary first year. His campaign to dismiss Hitchcock before his probationary year was up failed because of the testimonies of Walker, his field training officer, and Sergeants Breen and Baxter. The vindictive little Bostwick never forgot it.

Hitchcock took his seat at briefing. Because he was not one to follow the news, he was unprepared for Sergeant Breen's first announcement.

"All right—listen up. This is not for release to the public. The Medical Examiner called this afternoon. The decomposed body of a white male found by a couple deer hunters in the woods near the Issaquah-Hobart Road a couple days ago has been positively identified as that of Colin Wilcox, the convicted killer Hitchcock arrested at Charlie's a few weeks ago. The cause of death was a bullet to the back of the head, hands bound behind him, execution style. The King County dicks are investigating and since Wilcox was our arrest, ours will continue to be involved."

The news stunned Hitchcock.

Breen looked at Hitchcock. "Roger, you are to meet with county homicide dicks and ours at Captain Holland's office at 8 a.m., Monday. They want to talk to you about your arrest of Wilcox."

Returning his attention to his squad, Breen told his men, "Got a full moon tonight, and we know what that means — the crazies are out and the calls are heavy—the animals are tearing the city apart. Second shift has been swamped since sundown—get your gear and get out there—it'll be a long night. Be careful: I don't want anybody getting hurt. Dis-*missed!*"

While other officers left to get their gear, Hitchcock remained seated, mulling over the news of the execution. Whatever Wilcox's mission at Charlie's Place was, his failure became his death sentence. He had to be executed to ensure his silence. Stakes this high didn't jive with a blue-collar beer joint like Charlie's.

The place and manner of the Wilcox execution were a calculated message, the likes of which Hitchcock saw in villages in 'Nam, when he was on patrols; when the V.C. executed leaders and left the bodies to intimidate villagers from cooperating with the Americans or their allies. This message announced the deadly presence of a new wolf in the sheep pen; but few Americans would grasp it. *Time for a change in tactics*, Hitchcock told himself.

He remembered how the Army in 'Nam increased their effectiveness by developing reliable intelligence on enemy movements and strengths through friendly interaction with the civilian populace, even when they came to Phu Loi for medical attention. As a result the Army took the fight to the enemy, winning battles and saving lives. Hitchcock resolved to find his own mouse-in-the-corner, a mole—at least one. Hitchcock didn't know how to go about it, but he would do it, even if his mistakes got him fired. *A city this size next door to Seattle needs an intelligence unit like Seattle has, yet we don't even have a narc squad*, he thought.

His thoughts turned to the envelope. He opened it and read the note inside. What he read set him back. Though unsigned, he knew it was from Eve, who had gone to great risk to warn him he was being targeted, by whom and how and why. He found Walker in the hallway and took him aside.

"I need a favor. I'm supposed to meet Bostwick in his office now. *There will be trouble.* After I go in, stand outside the door and be my witness to everything that's said. Don't get caught."

Though surprised, Walker agreed. "Sure," he shrugged.

Hitchcock knocked on the Lieutenant's door "Come in Roger, and close the door," Bostwick ordered.

To be continued…

The saga continues in Book Two …

THE NEW DARKNESS

Order more books at
Amazon Books.com, or
www.bluesuitchronicles.com

Contact the Author at
John@bluesuitchronicles.com
Bluesuit Chronicles on Facebook
Google: John Hansen Historical Crime
Fiction Novels

Books by John Hansen

Song of the Waterwheel

The Bluesuit Chronicles Series:

The War Comes Home
The New Darkness
Valley of Long Shadows
Day Shift
Unfinished Business

Published and Award Winning Essays

Losing Kristene
Riding the Superstitions